WILDFIRE

WILDFIRE

A Flames to Ashes Novel

Hailey M. Bertoldi

For my beautiful Luna,
who inspired the heart of this story,
and the little café that began it all.

Kennedy

1

The smell of fresh coffee clung to my skin, a permanent side effect of owning the place I loved most. Luna's Hollow had been mine for three years, and every time I walked through its doors, I still felt that same spark of pride. It was mine. It was built from long nights, early mornings, and enough caffeine to kill a miniature horse—my labor of love, my dream, my world. More than just a café, it was a sanctuary—a cozy escape lined with towering bookshelves, soft candlelight, and the lingering scent of vanilla and worn pages—a place for kindred spirits to lose themselves in stories, coffee, and quiet magic. Though lately, the peace I'd built here felt fragile. Why? I don't know. I couldn't tell you, but it didn't feel right.

For whatever reason, today was a struggle for me. I glanced at the clock; its hands crawled at a painfully slow pace. With a sigh, I straightened as Mr. Ross approached the counter, his empty mug in hand. His silver hair and neatly trimmed beard framed his face, a face etched with the stories of a life well-lived. Not a single day had passed without Mr. Ross settling into his usual spot in the back corner, always within an hour before closing and always with a book. It was unusual, but he was kind, so I never thought much of it.

"You should slow down, Kennedy. You're always here, always working. Life has a way of slipping through your fingers when you're not looking." His words lingered, settling uncomfortably in my chest. I forced a smile, turning to grab the pot of dark roast coffee to fill his mug.

I leaned against the counter, rubbing a hand over my eyes as Sienna slid a to-go cup toward me. I jumped, still deep in thought as I processed Mr. Ross's words. "You know, for someone who owns a cafe, you sure do look like you could use some coffee."

Sienna Moretti had been my best friend since second grade. She was the only person who could read me like a book. She knew when I was tired, stressed, or about to make a questionable life decision. It was both a gift and a curse.

"Thanks, Sisi," I muttered, picking up the cup and taking a long sip without asking what was in it.

"Or a spa day. Or a sugar daddy." She added, wiggling her brows.

I choked on my drink, laughing as I wiped my mouth with the back of my hand. "Why settle for one when I can have all three?"

She grinned, flicking my arm with a bar towel before I returned to the espresso machine.

Sienna was right—I was beat.

Before I could take another sip, the café door flew open with a gust of crisp evening air. The little brass bell overhead jingled as the "infamous" Jaxon Fischer strode in, bringing his usual reckless energy with him. His dark jacket was unzipped, revealing a faded band tee, and his grin was already in place—charming and utterly full of shit.

Jaxon had always been like this—storming into rooms as if he owned them, leaving chaos in his wake. Taller than most, broad through the shoulders, he carried himself with a kind of careless swagger that bordered on arrogance. His dark hair was cut just short enough to look intentional, but always a little unkempt, as if he wanted people to believe he didn't care. And then there were his eyes—bright blue and restless, never still, scanning, calculating. They weren't warm, not really.

They burned too hot, like he was always two seconds away from turning that grin into something sharper.

"Good evening, ladies! Aren't we all looking absolutely divine today?"

Sienna and I exchanged an eye roll as he leaned dramatically against the counter, his smirk deepening like he could hear our internal groans.

"Before I say anything else, I require that drink. You know, the one with the little artsy pictures." He waved a lazy hand as if he were royalty, placing an order.

I huffed a quiet laugh but turned toward the espresso machine without protest. As the steam hissed and the scent of fresh coffee deepened, I glanced over my shoulder. "You know, for someone who refuses to learn the actual names of drinks, you sure are picky."

"Hey, I respect the craft," he shot back, tapping the counter for emphasis.

A minute later, I set his cappuccino down in front of him. Before I pulled my hand away, I leaned in with a smirk. "What kind of chaos are you dragging us into this time?"

Jaxon's eyes flickered with amusement as he mirrored my movement, closing the space between us like he was testing me, calling my bluff.

I held my ground briefly before pulling back, but my smirk remained.

"So," he started, straightening with a devilish grin. "I got invited to that new club that just opened up—The Veil or something like that. And, lucky for you two, I happen to have three VIP tickets." He fanned them out between his fingers like a winning hand in a poker game. "Thought you beauties might want to join me for a night out on the town!"

Sienna crossed her arms, giving him a skeptical look. "You have three VIP tickets, and you want to take us? Out of all the women in this city? What's in it for you?"

Jaxon's confidence faltered for a split second before he scoffed. "Come on, man. Why does there always have to be a catch? Look, y'all are single, right? And when was the last time you went out, Kennedy?" He gestured toward me with his cup. "This shop is eating up your social life. Let's have fun! Paint the town red or whatever my parents used to say."

He lifted his cappuccino and took a sip, completely unaware of the foam mustache left behind. I grinned and tapped my upper lip in silent warning. He frowned, confused, before realization hit. He wiped his mouth hastily, and Sienna and I burst into laughter.

"Paint the town red?" Sienna snorted. "What are you, fifty?"

Jaxon pressed his hand to his chest, eyes wide with faux offense. "Rude. My parents were very wise people."

I shook my head at their antics, but a night out actually sounded nice. It had been a while since I let myself have fun with my friends. They'd been amazing, helping out at the shop when I needed them, especially since I really only had one other employee. Maybe I owed them—and myself—a break.

Sienna, of course, wasn't about to make it easy. She leaned against the counter, arms crossed, looking every bit the negotiator.

"Alright, we'll go on one condition," Sienna said, pointing a finger at him. "You're covering everything. Uber, drinks…the works. Capiche?"

"Unbelievable," Jaxon groaned, dragging a hand down his face. "Fine, deal—but if you tell people I'm your gay cousin again, this will be your last free meal ticket, you greedy gremlin."

Laughter filled the café as the memory resurfaced—vivid, ridiculous, and ultimately us.

As the laughter settled, I found myself staring at the VIP tickets still fanned out in Jaxon's hand—a night out. Dancing, music, drinks, the kind of thing I used to love before life got too complicated. Before responsibility had me waking up at the crack of dawn to keep this place running.

I glanced around my café, the warm glow of the hanging lights bouncing off the espresso machine, the scent of roasted coffee beans calming me like it always did. I built this place from the ground up and poured everything I had into it. And yeah, maybe Jaxon had a point. Maybe, somewhere along the way, I'd let it consume me. Not that I regretted it. This shop saved me; it gave me something that was mine after years of feeling like I was just surviving. After my mom died, after my dad—well, after everything. I needed something to anchor me when the rest of my world was falling apart.

But anchors get heavy. And, for once, maybe I could let go—just a little.

I groaned, but deep down, warmth curled in my chest. It had been forever since I let myself go out just for fun. Maybe because, deep down, I was scared of how much I'd changed.

The old me would've jumped at the chance. The new me hesitated.

"Fine," I relented. "But if it sucks, I'm leaving early."

Sienna beamed. "Deal."

Jaxon tapped the counter. "We'll make sure you have fun." His smirk deepened like he knew exactly what he was doing. And, annoyingly, so did I. I hated that part of me still reacted to it, just a little.

Jaxon grinned. "I knew you couldn't resist me."

I laughed, shaking my head. "Let's just see if you survive the night with Sienna. She's got expensive taste, and now you're funding it."

His smirk faltered just slightly. "Maybe I should've set a budget..."

Sienna grabbed the tickets from his hand before he could change his mind. "Nope! Too late! Tonight, we ride!"

"Tomorrow," I corrected, shooting her a look. "I need one good night of sleep, and I have to give Izzy a heads-up that she's closing. At least twenty-four hours' notice, like a responsible adult." I sighed, already pulling out my phone to text her. If I didn't, I'd either have to close early or bail on the whole thing, and after all this build-up, that wasn't an option.

I slid it into my back pocket and flashed them both a smile before turning on my heel to start closing down the shop. I was exhausted and more than ready to go home. Luckily, the shop had emptied right before Jaxon arrived, so I quickly flipped the open sign so that it said closed, locked the door, and dimmed the lights.

As the glow softened, I caught Jaxon wiggling his brows at me, teasing as always. There was always this flirty tension between us, confusing, considering he was the one who ended things. Rolling my eyes, I swatted his arm playfully before slipping past him, making my way behind the counter to help Sienna with the last of the dishes.

"Are you going to make yourself useful, or just keep being a pest?" Sienna called out, eyeing Jaxon as he spun lazily back and forth in a counter chair.

Snapping out of his trance, he hopped up, grabbed the trash bags, and took them outside while Sienna and I finished the last of the closing tasks. When he returned, I offered them both a tired but grateful smile.

"Thanks for helping me today. Let's go home! And Sisi, come over tomorrow and help me get ready. I think I forgot how to dress like a girl."

We laughed before heading out the back and locking the door behind us. Wishing each other a good night, we closed out another night of my dream made real, no expense spared, including my sanity.

The drive home was quiet—the kind of silence that let my thoughts wander. By the time I pulled into my driveway, exhaustion had settled deep into my bones. Even unlocking the door felt like more effort than I had left to give, but the promise of my warm bed and my darling cat, Luna, kept me motivated. It's true, I'm 100% an old lady at heart. Give me a cozy couch, a soft blanket, and my cat over a night out any day.

But even old ladies needed to let loose once in a while. Besides, what was the worst that could happen? A hangover and a guilty conscience?

The warmth that escaped through the open door wrapped around me like a blanket, starkly contrasting the crisp night air outside. I stepped in willingly, shutting the door with a quiet click and locking it with ease. My eyes adjusted to the dim room, scanning for Luna, but I didn't have to search for long—her glowing green eyes found me first.

A postcard sat on the entryway floor.

My brows pulled together. Had I left it there earlier? I didn't remember seeing it when I left for work this morning.

I hesitated before picking it up, my fingertips tracing the worn edges.

The front displayed a beach I didn't recognize, waves rolling lazily under an overcast sky. It was the kind of scene that should've been calming, but something about it felt wrong. A pit formed in my stomach before I even flipped it over.

Then I saw the writing.

I won't let you slip away from me again, sweet girl. I've missed you.

No name. No return address. Just a tiny, hand-drawn heart.

I inhaled sharply, fingers clenching around the card stock before I could stop myself. My skin felt tight, my pulse hammering behind my ribs.

A chill rolled down my spine, slow and cold.

Sweet girl.

The words sat heavy in my chest, suffocating. I hadn't seen those words written in years, not since college.

Not since him.

My nightmare was never found, but because he stopped, I was presumed safe

The room around me blurred for a moment, memories pressing at the edges of my mind, threatening to drag me back. Crumpled postcards in my dorm mailbox. A presence I could never quite shake—the feeling of eyes on me when no one was there.

I swallowed hard and forced my grip to loosen.

No.

Not again.

Luna's soft chirp snapped me back to reality, her small body winding around my legs. I exhaled slowly, forcing my shoulders to relax.

It was just a postcard.

It didn't mean anything.

Except it did.

He found me.

I set it down on the entryway table, turning away from it.

Ignore it. Don't feed into it.

"There you are," I murmured, scooping her into my arms. Her soft fur pressed against my cheek as she let out a small, satisfied purr. I sighed as I held her tight, grounding myself in the simple comfort of her warmth.

When I reached for the light switch, I had already convinced myself it was nothing.

It was probably just a coincidence. It had to be.

My home was empty but not silent—the low hum of the TV played in the background, filling the quiet that would otherwise feel too heavy after a long day. I always left it on for Luna, though I wasn't sure if it was really for her sake or mine.

For a split second, I thought about calling Sienna, just to hear another voice, but what would I even say? That a piece of cardstock made my skin crawl? No. I wasn't that girl anymore. Still, every sound in the apartment felt sharper. Closer. Like the silence was listening.

Kicking off my shoes, I let out a slow breath, finally allowing my body to relax. The scent of fresh coffee still clung to my clothes, mixing with the faint lavender wax melt I'd left burning that morning. I was home. I was safe. Free to let the weight of the day slip from my shoulders. Squeezing Luna tight, I swallowed the lingering ache and poured myself a glass of wine, pretending the tightness in my chest wasn't fear. It was just a coincidence. It had to be.

Mr. Ross's words echoed in my head as I took off my shoes. *Life has a way of slipping through your fingers when you're not looking.* He hadn't meant anything by it, but the weight of the words settled deep. That's how it had felt with my mother—one moment, she was here, and then she wasn't. The cancer had taken her before I'd even figured out who I was, before I had the chance to ask all the questions I hadn't known I would have.

My father had always said grief was wasted energy, that there was no use in dwelling on what couldn't be changed. Maybe that was why I had stopped expecting anything from him. He existed in my life only in name, a man of power and influence that had never extended beyond the superficial. I had built my own life and stability without relying on him. And yet, sometimes, I wondered if there had ever been a version of him that could have been more nurturing.

I absently stroked Luna's fur as I walked through the apartment, flipping on a few lamps to chase away the dimness. The space was mine, built on my terms, separate from the shadow of my father's name. He would never understand a quiet night like this, he only understood power and control. I had carved out something different for myself, something he had no part in.

I went through the motions—feeding Luna, washing off the day in a steaming shower, slipping into my favorite worn-in t-shirt. By the time I climbed into bed, exhaustion pressed heavily against my limbs, though my thoughts refused to quiet.

The postcard sat untouched where I'd left it.

I turned over, willing myself to sleep, but as I closed my eyes, a thought crept in, cold and unshakable.

He's back.

I swallowed, my chest tightening. The thought burrowed deep, an unwanted presence refusing to let go. I told myself it was impossible, but the words felt thin—fragile, like they could splinter under their own weight.

The house felt quieter than usual. Too quiet.

Luna purred against my chest as my arms wrapped around her. Her warmth and vibrations helped ground me, pulling me back to the moment.

I exhaled. Tomorrow would come like it always did.

And still, as I let my eyes drift closed, I knew something had already shifted.

Kennedy

2

The dreaded night had arrived.

Funny how "a night out" always sounded better hours before I actually had to put on real clothes and pretend to be social.

I stood in front of my full-length mirror, tugging at the hem of my dress and feeling more frumpy than ever. I sighed, shifting my weight as I posed in different outfits, hoping one of them would magically make me feel like I belonged in a club. Each one was uglier than the last—or maybe that was just my mood talking.

My gaze drifted to my closet, landing on the untouched row of heels neatly stacked on the shelves. I had more pairs than I was comfortable admitting; a past version of myself convinced me they were essential.

Now, they just gather dust. I couldn't even remember the last time I wore any of them. A lifetime ago, maybe.

Before I could change into sweats and call it a night, the front door slammed shut.

"Alright, let's see it," Sienna's voice rang through the apartment before I even reached the handle. She shoved the door open, her sharp eyes immediately scanning my outfit like a drill sergeant inspecting her troops.

I groaned. "Just say it."

"That's a hell no."

She marched straight past me, already heading for my closet. Hangers clattered as she dove in, tossing fabric left and right like a woman on a mission.

"Why did I even ask you to help?" I grumbled, dodging a rogue sleeve.

Sienna shot me a smirk over her shoulder. "Because you have no idea how to dress for a night out. And because I refuse to let you embarrass me in public."

I grabbed a pillow and launched it at her head, but she ducked quickly. "Remind me again why we're even doing this?"

"Because you need to live a little, babe. And because Jaxon and I already made a pact to drag your ass out, so there's no backing out now."

I sighed, flopping onto my bed. There was no fighting it—she was relentless.

Sienna sifted through my closet, her reactions growing more exaggerated with every piece she shoved aside: a scoff, a dramatic sigh, a full-body cringe. She yanked out a dress, held it up to the light, and visibly recoiled before tossing it over her shoulder. Then, suddenly, she froze.

I propped myself up on my elbows, dreading whatever chaos she was about to unleash. Then I saw how her cheeks lifted, her lips curving into a devilish smile.

"Oh, God. What did you find?" My heart began to race.

She turned slowly, eyes glinting with mischief. "Oh, nothing…"

I groaned, already knowing whatever she picked would have me looking like the classiest whore you'll ever see.

In her hand was a long-sleeved red mini dress with a deep plunge in the neckline. I'd bought it during a brief moment of delusion—back when I thought confidence could be purchased if the dress was tight enough. It still had the tag.

"My titties will be greeting people before I even get the chance to," I muttered, taking the dress from her with a sigh, trying to hold back a yawn.

"Bitch, if you don't smile and wake the hell up, I swear to God!" Sienna shoved the dress into my hands, kissed my cheek, and practically skipped across the room to grab the TV remote. A second later, music blasted through the speakers, sealing my fate.

I couldn't help it—I felt terrible leaving the shop completely in Izzy's hands, so I slipped in to help open it. I probably should've just let her handle it, but the place felt too quiet without me this morning. At least this way, I wasn't taking the whole night off. Izzy only had to close, and I wouldn't have to spend the entire night worrying about the shop.

The music—I couldn't lie—put me in a mood. Something about it allowed my body to loosen up, the tension melting from my shoulders as the beat pulsed through the room. For the first time all day, excitement sparked in my chest.

With my newfound enthusiasm, I slipped into the dress. My hair and makeup were already done—thankfully, I had finished before Sienna even arrived—so all that was left was to take in the final result.

I turned to the mirror and froze for a second. The reflection looking back at me didn't feel like the tired, overworked version I usually saw. My curls—deep red, bright even under the dim light—framed my face in soft spirals, healthy and unruly in a way I secretly loved. My green-hazel eyes looked sharper, brighter, and the freckles scattered across my fair skin only made them stand out more. The dress hugged in all the right places, reminding me of the curves I usually tried not to think about.

I wasn't used to staring. But for once, I had to admit—I looked...nice. Maybe even more than nice.

The moment didn't last long. Sienna waltzed in with two pregame shots, setting them down with a grin before wrapping her arms around me from behind.

"Look at you, bitch. You're so hot! Now, let's add the finishing touch."

Her eyes flicked to my shoe closet before she let me go, practically skipping toward the heels she had in mind. I didn't even need to look—I already knew.

When she spun around, holding my black-red-bottoms like they were the Holy Grail, I groaned.

"You hate me."

"I love you," she corrected. "I just hate those tired-ass flats you always wear."

Sighing, I made the ultimate sacrifice, slipping on the heels that would inevitably cut my night short. I looked damn good, but let's be honest—these wouldn't be on long, or I'd be drinking way more than planned to get through it.

With the outfit complete, Sienna grinned, holding up our shots like a toast was in order. I grabbed mine, pausing for a moment to take her in. She looked every bit like the troublemaker she was—black crop tube top, tight black mini skirt, and leather boots that screamed terrible decisions were about to be made. Her legs were endless, toned and smooth, carrying her with that reckless kind of confidence that always got us both into trouble. That ridiculous, enviable brown hair spilled in a glossy sheet down her back, almost to her waist, a curtain she wielded like a weapon without even trying. Her skin held a warm olive tone no California summer could compete with, and those golden-brown eyes sparked with mischief, daring the world to try and tame her.

"You look hot," I admitted, tilting my shot glass toward her.

She smirked. "I know. But not as hot as you. Now, shut up and drink."

I rolled my eyes but clinked my glass against hers before throwing the shot back, feeling the warmth in my chest. Tonight was happening, whether I was ready or not.

Suddenly, the door swung open with a sharp creak.

"Well, well, well…" Jaxon's voice rang out, full of playful surprise, his eyes drinking in my outfit with an almost teasing glint. He leaned casually against the doorframe, arms crossed, taking his time as if savoring the moment. "I didn't think you had it in you, Kennedy. But damn, look at you."

His gaze lingered a little too long, and I felt the heat rise in my cheeks as his words hit a little too close to the mark. Sienna shot him a quick look, but he just flashed a grin her way, not even trying to hide how impressed he was.

"You're gonna make me look bad, aren't you?" Jaxon's voice was low, his grin still in place, but his eyes lingered on me a little too long, and something in his gaze made my stomach flutter.

"As a matter of fact, she's always made you look bad." Sienna shot back with a playful smile before grabbing my hand and spinning me around to show me off.

The sudden motion gave me a chance to regain my composure. I closed my eyes for a moment, letting the world spin around me, and when it finally stopped, I smirked.

Jaxon's expression faltered slightly as I tried to hide my face from him.

"The car's waiting outside. Don't worry, Sisi, there's a bottle in the car, but we should get going!" Jaxon's voice was filled with that confident, commanding tone he always used when he wanted to take charge. He quickly ushered us toward the door, and I grabbed my bag and phone, following Sienna out of the room.

Jaxon hesitated in the entryway, looking down at the wooden table. Before I could question what he was doing, Sienna was already pulling me toward the door, eager to get us out.

In true Jaxon fashion, a flashy white SUV limo was waiting to take us on the grand adventure he'd promised. Sienna squealed with excitement while I rolled my eyes, already bracing myself for the over-the-top antics I knew were coming. The driver opened the door with a practiced smile, offering a rundown of the beverages available before stepping aside to let us climb in.

I was the first to slide into the plush interior, making room for the others as they followed. My eyes immediately landed on the tequila bottle. Perfect, I thought, reaching for it with a grin. I didn't even ask if anyone wanted tequila—I was pouring it, and that's what they were getting. Pouring myself a double shot, I caught Jaxon's surprised expression.

"Damn, let's go, Jessica Rabbit! Someone's ready to party! To Kennedy!" Jaxon laughed, raising his shot glass high. Sienna and I clinked our glasses with his, and I was taken aback at the fact that he'd used the nickname he'd once called me when we were dating, but I chose to let it go. We all threw back the shot, and my eyes squeezed shut as the tequila burn hit me full force. I hated the taste, but it was my go-to drink for any uncomfortable situation.

The music blared, and lights flashed in every color, making it feel like we were already in a club. We shared a few more drinks on the way, and by the time we pulled up to The Veil, I was the perfect amount of tipsy.

Sienna tugged gently at my hand, guiding me out of the limo and toward the crowd. Jaxon led us to the front of the line, handing his VIP tickets to the bouncer. They exchanged a nod, and the bouncer moved aside, giving us a wink as he directed us inside. Sienna and I giggled at the gesture, our hands instinctively interlacing as we followed Jaxon inside.

The moment we stepped through the doors, the energy hit us. The music's bass thumped in my chest, vibrating through the dark, pulsing lights. The air was thick with perfume, sweat, and the electric hum of people having fun. Bodies moved in a chaotic rhythm on the dance floor while others crowded the bar, laughter and voices blending with the music. Neon signs flickered, casting an almost surreal glow across the room, and I could feel the weight of the night ahead pressing in with anticipation.

"I'll grab us some drinks!" Jaxon offered, his voice barely audible over the beat, and we both nodded in acknowledgment.

I was feeling good. Instead of standing there waiting for Jaxon, I had this sudden urge to dance. Tugging Sienna out onto the dance floor, we both laughed, losing ourselves to the rhythm. It felt like I was finally letting go, letting all my worries drift away with the fog that swirled around our bodies. The music moved through me, and my hips swayed in ways I hadn't even remembered I could move.

Suddenly, I felt a presence behind me, a body pressing against mine, and Sienna's expression shifted just slightly. I turned around to find Jaxon holding our drinks.

His gaze flickered over my shoulder, scanning the crowd like he'd just noticed something off.

"Here you go, Red," he said, handing me my Tequila Sunrise, but something was distracting about how he said it.

I flashed a grin, pretending not to notice. Jaxon always had a way of making things about himself, but this was different—his usual smugness was subdued, as if his attention was elsewhere.

Ignoring it, I took my drink and spun toward a nearby cocktail table.

Thinking Sienna and Jaxon would follow, I pivoted, only to find them standing in the same spot. They looked like they were arguing, with Sienna gripping his wrist tightly and her lips pressed into a frustrated line.

I sighed. Typical. Choosing to ignore them, I let the music take over again, allowing myself to scan the room for some eye candy.

That's when I felt it.

A shift in the air. It was like someone had just walked into the room and changed the atmosphere without saying a word.

My attention snapped to a man standing at the bar, casually leaning against it with a drink in hand. He wasn't doing anything special, yet somehow, he commanded attention from me and the space around him.

He had a bit of a shaggy beard and most definitely needed a haircut, but his eyes... His eyes were breathtaking and piercing all at once. At six feet two inches, he stood with an athletic build and what looked like tattoos peeking from his sleeves. But his eyes had already stolen my attention, and I chose to ignore the rest of his physique.

I quickly looked away, realizing I'd been staring. I shook my head, telling myself it was just the atmosphere, the lighting, the music—it was making everyone feel a little more intense tonight. Still, I couldn't help but glance back, the pull toward him stronger than it should have been.

He was still watching me. Not in the way most men at a club did. His gaze wasn't hungry, wasn't lazy with drunken attraction. No, this was different—focused. Measured. I turned my head again, the realization hitting me that I was getting far too caught up in his gaze as if it had some kind of magnetic pull on me.

I didn't know who he was, but something about him stuck in my mind like a puzzle piece I couldn't quite place.

Something old. Something unsettling.

Forgetting I was in public and that he was an actual human being, I realized too late that I'd lingered too long on him.

That's when he moved.

Not rushed, not eager—just smooth, fluid, like he had already planned this moment long before I noticed him. His eyes locked onto mine like he'd decided it was time to close the distance.

I practically choked on the drink in my hand, nervously stirring it with my straw as his green eyes again held me captive. Clearing my throat, I offered an unwarranted, flirty smile as I tried to recover.

"Listen, I know you're not just a pretty face, but those eyes…" I blurted, fully aware of how I was probably staring at him, like he was a piece of meat.

And then, I swear I heard angels singing. Not literally. But the way his lips curved slightly, the ghost of amusement flickering in those green eyes, made my pulse stutter. Not a full smile. Not a smirk. Just the barest hint of knowing.

He chuckled, and it wasn't the awkward, pitying laugh. No, this was genuine amusement, like he thought my awkwardness was part of the show, like he expected.

I couldn't decide if he was laughing at me because I was a little mentally challenged, blurting out random compliments to strangers, or if my line was the smoothest he'd ever heard. I was voting for the latter.

Before I could say anything to make matters stranger, he glanced down at my drink, and this man, this stranger, dared to scoff at me before flagging down the bartender.

"Are you drinking anything, or do you just enjoy spinning ice around in a glass with your straw?"

I shouldn't have found the teasing so attractive.

Of course, I was drinking something, I thought to myself. But as I looked down at my empty glass, I pursed my lips and shrugged.

"Tequila Sunrise, please."

He raised an eyebrow, clearly unimpressed with my empty glass. "Tequila, huh? Bold choice." He turned to the bartender, giving a slight nod. His movements were effortless, as if he were used to being listened to. "Make it a double and hold the judgment."

I wasn't sure if I was more impressed with his confidence or that he could make such a simple request sound like an art form. Still, I rolled with it, leaning back just enough to keep the tension alive—no need to bring out the strong, independent woman just yet. Instead, I gave him a smirk, letting the playful energy keep us both on edge.

"You're buying, right?"

He met my smirk with a knowing look, and for a second, it felt like he already knew how I'd respond before I even said it.

It was a weird, electrifying sensation.

"For you? Always."

And there it was. I wasn't sure if I was annoyed or intrigued by how comfortable he was in his skin, but something about the way he said it made my stomach do that little flip again.

We talked for what felt like hours, drink after drink, laugh after laugh. The music, the conversation—it all blurred together until it was just me and him, lost in this magnetic pull. The atmosphere felt charged, like the whole world had faded away as he kept me locked in that gaze, making me feel like I was the only thing that mattered in this room full of people.

How did he make it feel like we were the only two people here?

But then, I felt it—a shift, like the air in the room, thickened. Like a thread of tension had been plucked, reverberating through the moment.

Out of the corner of my eye, I saw Jaxon pushing through the crowd, with concern written all over his face. Behind him, Sienna was trying to pull him back, her hand on his arm, her eyes rolling as she became more frustrated with his attitude.

"Kennedy," Sienna said, sliding up beside me with an apologetic grin. "I'm sorry, I tried to keep him away, but you know Jaxon."

I shot her a look, half-amused, half-exasperated. "Not very good at that, I see?"

"Listen," she started, smirking, "he saw you talking to someone and couldn't let it go."

Jaxon's voice cut through then—too casual, too playful for the tension that had built up between me and the stranger who had somehow taken over my attention.

"Hey, Red. Who's this joker?"

For a moment, the man across from me didn't even acknowledge Jaxon. He held my gaze, his lips curling into a slow, deliberate smile. Not smug. Not arrogant. Just calculated.

Like he knew something the rest of us didn't.

Then, finally, he turned his attention to Jaxon. But rather than looking irritated, he looked entertained.

"Do you always open with insults, or just when feeling threatened?"

His voice was smooth, laced with amusement, but there was a distinct undertone—one that suggested he wasn't taking Jaxon seriously, not even a little bit.

Jaxon's smirk twitched, but he held his ground. "Funny. You just looked like you were overstaying your welcome."

The green-eyed man flicked his gaze back to me, his unreadable expression sending a slow chill down my spine. He studied me, not in a way that felt rushed or reactionary, but deliberate.

Calculated.

Then, with that same maddening ease, he shifted his attention back to Jaxon, finally acknowledging him with a slight tilt of his head.

"And you look like you're trying a little too hard," he mused, voice smooth as whiskey.

Jaxon stiffened, jaw tightening. "Yeah? I don't remember you being invited to our night out."

The stranger didn't even blink. If anything, his lips curved slightly, like Jaxon's challenge amused him.

"I wasn't aware I needed an invitation." His eyes flicked to me again, assessing. "But from where I'm standing, it seems I was welcomed just fine."

Jaxon huffed a sharp breath, stepping forward just enough to put himself between us. I could feel the tension radiating off of him, thick and unrelenting. But the man who had my attention all night? He was completely, infuriatingly calm.

And somehow, that made it worse.

Jaxon squared his shoulders. "If you think you're gonna—"

The man in control exhaled through his nose, almost disappointed.

"You talk too much."

The words weren't sharp or loud, but they cut through the space between them like a blade, so effortless and dismissive that it made Jaxon bristle.

I barely had a second to process before the stranger leaned in, so close I could feel the warmth of his breath against my cheek.

"You seemed to be enjoying my company just fine," he murmured loud enough for Jaxon to hear.

Jaxon shifted beside me, his fists clenching at his sides. But the man in control still wasn't looking at him. His eyes were on me.

I felt caught, trapped in something unspoken. Something dangerous.

Sienna must have sensed it because she slid her arm through mine, her voice sharp and irritated.

"Jesus, Jaxon. You might as well put your dick right on the table!"

Jaxon's glare didn't waver. But the green-eyed stranger, without another glance, reached for my hand.

My breath stalled as his fingers—warm, firm, unshaken—lifted mine.

And then he kissed my knuckles.

Slow. Purposeful. Like he was sealing a promise.

I barely registered my own sharp inhale, my skin burning where his lips had been.

Then, finally, his gaze flicked back up to mine, something unreadable flickering in his eyes.

"We'll see each other again, Ms. Royal."

Everything in me locked up.

My name.

I hadn't told him my name, let alone my last name.

Before I could form a single thought, he was already gone, melting into the crowd like he'd never been there.

And I was left standing in the middle of the club, my pulse hammering in my ears, my mind reeling.

I stared after him, my mind still reeling from the encounter, when I felt the irritation building up inside me. Jaxon didn't hesitate. His voice sliced through the air, sharp and annoyed. "What the hell was that about?"

I spun to face him, the frustration bubbling up. "What the hell was that about?" I repeated. "Are you actually kidding me right now, Jaxon? We're at a club; I was socializing. What the hell did you think it was?" I snapped, my voice colder than I intended.

He interrupted me, yanked me out of something that had been, admittedly, a little intense—but damn, it had felt real.

Jaxon frowned, his posture stiff, clearly thrown off by my reaction. His lips parted like he had something else to say, but Sienna let out a sharp laugh before he could, shaking her head in disbelief.

"Oh my God, Jaxon. Go take a lap before your ego collapses in on itself."

Jaxon snapped his gaze to her, his jaw flexing, but she wasn't done. She gestured toward me, her brows lifting. "Look at her! Do you see her smiling right now? Nah, you fucked up, and you know it."

Jaxon exhaled through his nose, rubbing the back of his neck like he was debating whether or not to push back.

His jaw ticked. "Fine. Whatever. I'm getting a drink."

With a half-shrug, he turned, pushing through the crowd. But not before glancing over his shoulder—one last look at me, unreadable. But there was something else there. A hesitation. A warning.

"Good idea, grab us one too!" Sienna called after him, completely unfazed.

The second he was gone, she turned toward me, her smirk dropping. "Okay, but for real—what the hell was that?"

I exhaled sharply, anger still buzzing under my skin.

"Are you serious? You two were arguing. Was I supposed to just stand there and wait for you guys to get it together?"

I shook my head, heat still rising to my face. "I don't care who I was talking to. Jaxon needs to mind his business."

Sienna clicked her tongue, arms crossing. "Yeah, no, that was some next-level bullshit."

She let out a dry laugh, shaking her head. "Like, babe, I know he's got issues, but Jesus Christ. He could've just peed on you to mark his territory and saved us all some time."

I let out a sharp breath, but I wasn't in the mood to laugh yet. My heart was still pounding, irritation simmering beneath the ghost of something else.

Sienna nudged me. "Seriously, though. Who was he?"

His voice. His touch. My last name on his lips.

My pulse was still thrumming, my fingers tingling where his had been.

A part of me wanted to shake it off, let it go. But I couldn't.

Something about him stuck.

I swallowed, realizing I never even got his name.

"...I have no idea."

Kennedy

3

About a week had passed since our sorry excuse for a night out. Jaxon and I hadn't spoken since the painfully silent drive home. Not for a lack of trying on his part—he'd reached out more times than I cared to count, trying to rehash the night, trying to justify himself. But I had no interest in rehashing anything. His behavior had been weird, inappropriate, possessive—and the more I thought about it, the angrier I got. I wasn't his anymore. I hadn't been his for years. And yet, for some reason, he still acted like he had a say in my life.

Although I won't lie, my mind kept drifting back to my mystery man.

The shop was unexpectedly busy for a Thursday. From the moment we opened, it had been all hands on deck. Thankfully, Sienna had decided to help out—because if she hadn't, I wasn't sure Izzy and I would have survived the crowd.

But something about her felt off.

Usually, Sienna was sassy, upbeat, and effortlessly put together. The kind of girl who always had a witty comeback and never left the house without at least a swipe of mascara. But lately... she'd been quieter, more focused. She still showed up, still helped out, but something was missing. The sparkle. The fire.

Even today, she hadn't bothered with makeup—not that she needed it. She was beautiful without it. But that wasn't the point.

It wasn't like her.

I wiped down the counter between orders, sneaking a glance at her as she frothed milk for a latte. She caught me looking and arched a brow.

"What?"

I shrugged. "Nothing. You just seem... different lately.

She rolled her eyes, passing off the drink to a customer before refocusing on me. "I could say the same about you."

I huffed a small laugh. "I've been the same."

Sienna shot me a look. "You haven't talked to Jaxon in, what? A week? That's not *the same.*"

I busied myself wiping the counter, but she wasn't letting it go.

"So... are you gonna?" she pressed. "Talk to him?"

I let out a slow breath. "No."

Sienna frowned. "Come on, Kennedy. You guys have been through worse fights than this. Just hear him out."

I opened my mouth to shut her down, but then—

I turned to grab a fresh rag when a flicker of memory hit me—Jaxon standing by my entry table that night, fingers grazing the edge of something.

My stomach dipped.

The postcard.

Have I seen it since then?

Before I could think too much about it, the bell above the door jingled, pulling my attention to a new customer.

I shook off the thought. Didn't matter. Not now.

I pursed my lips, shaking my head. Maybe I was just reading too much into things.

"I don't have anything to say to Jaxon," I said finally, brushing off the weird feeling. "And I don't really care what he has to say to me, either."

Sienna sighed, but thankfully, she didn't push it.

The shop was finally slowing down. The morning rush had bled into the lunch crowd, but now, in that brief lull before the mid-afternoon caffeine seekers started trickling in, I could finally breathe.

Steam hissed from the espresso machine as I wiped down the counter, falling into the familiar rhythm of the shop—grind, pull, steam, pour, repeat. The scent of coffee lingered heavily in the air, mixing with the faint sweetness of vanilla and caramel from the syrups lined up along the back wall.

Izzy was handling the register, her usual efficiency cutting through orders like clockwork, while Sienna leaned lazily against the counter, stirring her iced coffee with the same straw she'd been chewing on for the last fifteen minutes.

"You look like you're ready to pass out," she noted, her sharp gaze flicking up to mine.

I huffed, stretching out my sore arms. "I've been working all morning while you've been... supervising."

She snorted. "Hey, moral support is important."

Izzy slid a drink across the counter, sighing dramatically. "She's right, you know. I would've walked out hours ago if Sienna hadn't been standing here, doing absolutely nothing."

Sienna gasped, clutching her chest. "Wow. Betrayed in my own home."

I rolled my eyes but smiled anyway, feeling some of the tension from the last week ease off my shoulders. This—this was what I needed. Work. Routine. Something normal.

I turned to stack some fresh cups near the espresso machine, mind already drifting toward the next wave of orders, when—

A feeling.

Not a noise. Not a shift in the air. Just… something. A pull.

I glanced up toward the front of the shop, but there was nothing out of the ordinary—just a few customers lingering at their tables, the sound of a laptop keyboard clicking away, soft conversation humming underneath the indie music playing overhead.

Maybe I was imagining things.

I shook it off, refocusing on the machine in front of me, but the feeling didn't shake me.

Something was off.

I turned again, slower this time, my eyes scanning the café more carefully.

Nothing.

Still, the unease crawled along my spine, settling into the base of my stomach like a warning I couldn't quite place.

And then, just as I started to convince myself I was being ridiculous—

The door chime rang.

At first, I didn't even bother looking up. Just another customer. Just another person walking in for a caffeine fix, like any other day.

But the shift in the room was immediate.

I felt it before I saw it.

A prickle of awareness along my skin. A pause in the air, thick and heavy, stretching out like an invisible thread pulling tight.

I lifted my gaze—and froze.

Him.

The stranger from the club.

The green-eyed man who had left me spinning, who had walked away with my name on his lips like he'd known it long before I told him.

He stood just inside the doorway, hands tucked casually into the pockets of his jacket, his posture relaxed, effortless—like he belonged here. Like he was supposed to be here.

But he wasn't.

Not really.

I shouldn't have recognized him this fast. Shouldn't have felt this sharp jolt in my chest just from seeing him again.

And yet, there he was.

Here.

My pulse quickened, the breath I had been holding spilling out in a slow, steady exhale.

His gaze slid over the shop, taking in the space around him, before finally—inevitably—locking onto me.

And just like that, the room felt smaller.

His lips curved into something unreadable, something too smooth to be accidental. A small nod. A flicker of recognition.

Like this had been planned.

Like he'd been waiting for this.

I swallowed hard, gripping the rag in my hand a little too tightly, suddenly aware of the warmth lingering along my skin. Sienna, oblivious to the sudden change in atmosphere, nudged my hip. "Looks like someone couldn't get enough of you."

I barely registered her voice.

Because the green-eyed man had just started walking toward me.

And I wasn't sure if I wanted him to stop.

Or if I wanted him to keep going.

I tried to keep my composure, offering him a smile—polite, neutral, something safe. But the moment his eyes locked onto mine, that same unsettling, magnetic pull from the club wrapped around me like a vice.

His lips curved just slightly, not quite a smirk, but something close. "Kennedy." He said my name like it was a secret, something meant only for him.

A slow, nervous energy coiled in my stomach. "I didn't think I'd see you again."

"Didn't you?" His tone was unreadable. "I told you, you would. Guess you didn't believe me." He shrugged, a quiet chuckle following.

Sienna, still blissfully unaware of the way my pulse had started to hammer in my throat, leaned against the counter, grinning. "Guess you must've made quite the impression."

My fingers curled around the rag I'd been holding, the fabric damp between my hands. I had questions. So many questions. Like how he knew my name. Like, why did it feel like he was expecting this?

But I didn't ask them.

Because somehow, his presence filled the space between us so completely that I forgot how to form the words.

Clearing my throat, I finally set the rag down, realizing too late that my fingers had cramped from gripping it too tightly.

"Well, I'd get myself into trouble if I believed every stranger I met." My voice was steady, confidence threading through the words, even as my pulse betrayed me.

I didn't look away.

He leaned in, closing the space between us just enough to make it feel private. Deliberate.

"Trouble isn't always a bad thing, love."

His voice was low, rich, rolling off his tongue in a way that felt too smooth, too intentional. Like he knew exactly what effect he had on people.

I refused to give him the satisfaction.

I exhaled through my nose, unimpressed. "That depends on who's causing the trouble."

A deep chuckle left him. "Fair point." He studied me for a moment, eyes flicking over my face like he was piecing something together. "But I have a feeling you like a little trouble."

I lifted a brow, letting the silence stretch between us just long enough to make him wonder if I was going to respond.

Then, with the smallest smirk, I reached for a rag and started wiping the counter. "I have a feeling you like hearing yourself talk."

This time, his smile reached his eyes.

He didn't push. Didn't rush. Just reached into his jacket and pulled out his phone, setting it on the counter between us with the screen open to a new contact page.

A silent request.

I didn't move.

Instead, I lifted my gaze to his, unblinking. "You're pretty confident for a guy whose name I don't even know."

His fingers drummed against the counter once, slow and rhythmic. "I don't think you would've let me get this far if you weren't at least curious."

I rolled my lips together, considering him for half a second before picking up the phone. I typed my number in, but instead of handing it back, I slid it across the counter, just slightly out of reach.

His lips twitched, amused.

Before he could grab it, the shop door swung open, and the cool spring breeze followed.

I looked up just as Jaxon walked in.

His posture was relaxed, but his sharp blue eyes locked onto the scene in front of him.

Me. The stranger. The phone still sitting between us.

His gaze darkened.

For the briefest moment, I felt something uncomfortable coil low in my stomach.

The stranger. He still didn't have a name—moved first. His fingers wrapped around the phone, slipping it into his pocket as he slowly turned toward Jaxon.

Jaxon took a few measured steps forward, his expression unreadable. "Didn't realize we were handing out numbers with the coffee now."

Sienna, who had been very happily ignoring the sudden pissing contest, snapped her head up at that. Her brows lifted. "Oh, for fuck's sake," she muttered under her breath, loud enough for me to hear but not loud enough for Jaxon to care.

She took a long, slow sip of her coffee, then turned to Izzy at the register.

"Wanna place bets on who throws the first punch?"

Izzy, who had been pretending not to watch, coughed into her sleeve.

My irritation flared. "Jaxon."

He ignored me, his attention fixed on the man standing beside me.

The stranger remained composed, watching Jaxon as if he were mildly entertained. Then, instead of answering, he reached for a napkin and a pen from the counter.

He scribbled something down.

Then, with an effortless flick of his wrist, he smoothed out the napkin and slid it toward me.

My stomach twisted.

His green eyes locked onto mine, a slow, knowing smirk forming at the corner of his lips.

"I'll see you soon, Kennedy."

Then, as if he had all the time in the world, he turned and strolled toward the door.

Jaxon's jaw flexed as he tracked his movements, his fingers twitching at his sides.

The bell above the door jingled, and then he was gone.

For a long second, neither of us moved.

Then—

Jaxon exhaled sharply through his nose, his hand running through his hair in frustration.

I knew that move.

He wasn't just irritated. He was trying to calm himself down.

"Alright," he muttered. "I'm just gonna say it."

I crossed my arms. "Oh, great. I was worried you'd hold back."

His jaw clenched for half a second, but then he shook his head. "Look, I came here to—"

He sighed, rubbing the back of his neck. "I came here to apologize."

That threw me off. I had been ready for a fight. Not this.

Jaxon pressed his lips together before continuing. "I was outta line the other night. I know that. I don't—" He exhaled again, shaking his head. "I don't know what the hell came over me."

I narrowed my eyes. "Jealousy."

His gaze flicked up to mine. He didn't deny it.

"I just—" He ran a hand down his face. "I don't want you getting caught up with the wrong people, alright?"

A bitter laugh escaped before I could stop it. "And you get to decide who the 'wrong people' are?"

He took a slow, measured breath, his blue eyes searching mine. "You don't even know him."

That was it. That was my breaking point.

Sienna, who had been stirring her iced coffee like she wasn't witnessing a full-blown soap opera in real time, let out a sharp sigh. "Oh my God, are we really doing this *here*?" She looked around pointedly. "In the middle of the shop?"

At least three customers were very obviously eavesdropping, their drinks untouched as they tried to act like they were minding their business.

One woman pretended to scroll through her phone but didn't even blink.

Another guy at a corner table lowered his newspaper just enough to watch.

Sienna waved a hand in front of them. "I know y'all have lives. Go live them."

No one moved.

She huffed. "Unbelievable."

But I barely registered her, my focus locked onto Jaxon. His words still rang in my ears, fueling the fire already burning in my chest.

I scoffed, throwing my hands up. "Oh, but you do? You talked to him for what? Five seconds? And now you're an expert on who I should and shouldn't talk to?"

Jaxon's jaw tightened. "I don't need to know him, Kennedy. I know guys like him."

"Oh, guys like him?" My voice sharpened. "And what exactly does that mean? Because from where I'm standing, it sounds a lot like you're pissed off just because he talked to me."

His eyes flashed. "You think this is about me being pissed off?"

"Yeah, Jaxon. I do." I folded my arms tightly. "You're acting like you still have some kind of claim over me. You don't. You don't get to tell me who I can and can't talk to. Get a grip."

Sienna sucked in a breath through her teeth.

"Whew. That's gonna sting."

Jaxon visibly clenched his jaw, nostrils flaring.

Sienna slowly reached for her drink, whispering to Izzy, "This is about to get *so much worse*."

Izzy didn't respond—she was still watching like this was peak reality TV.

Jaxon held my gaze, the muscle in his jaw flexing like he was *physically* biting back whatever was on the tip of his tongue.

A few seconds of silence stretched between us.

Then, finally, his voice came out low. Controlled. "Just be careful, alright?"

I shook my head, letting out a sharp laugh. "I'll be fine, Dad."

Jaxon's lips pressed into a tight line, but he didn't say anything else.

Then, as I looked down, I saw the napkin and hesitated. Instead of reading it, I left it on the counter, turning away to grab a lid for a customer's drink.

Jaxon didn't move, but I could feel him watching me.

I busied myself with the order, trying to push down the lingering heat that still clung to my skin from the stranger's presence. I could still hear the faint jingle of the bell from when he left, could still feel the weight of his gaze even though he was long gone.

Behind me, there was a pause.

A beat of hesitation.

Then, the faintest click.

By the time I turned back around, Jaxon was standing exactly where I left him, hands stuffed casually into his pockets. The napkin still sat on the counter, untouched.

But something in his expression had changed.

"What?" I asked, forcing myself to focus.

Jaxon's lips pressed into a tight line, but then he just shrugged. "Nothing. Just—this guy. Something about him is off."

I crossed my arms, already annoyed. "Seriously, can we not keep doing this?"

His gaze flicked toward the door before landing back on me, something unreadable in his eyes. "You don't know what this guy is capable of."

I opened my mouth to argue, but I stopped.

Because the truth was—I didn't.

Not really.

Jaxon exhaled sharply, running a hand through his hair before shaking his head. "Just trying to look out for you."

I didn't respond. I just held his gaze, jaw tight.

With one last look at me, he sighed, obviously defeated, and turned to walk out the door.

The moment he was gone, I closed my eyes to take a second in the darkness behind my lids. When I opened them, I saw the note on the counter and picked it up. The napkin felt thin between my fingers, the ink slightly smudged, like he had written it without much thought—without caring if it looked neat.

I read it.

Next time, I want you all to myself.

My stomach twisted.

Heat curled low in my belly, slow and deliberate, a match striking against dry wood.

The weight of it sat heavily in my palm, the handwriting unfamiliar but bold.

Not rushed. Not careless. Intentional.

I exhaled through my nose, pressing my lips together as I folded the napkin back up.

Out of sight, out of mind.

Sienna arched a brow. "You're *keeping* it?" Her gaze flicked between me and the napkin, something unreadable in her expression.

I exhaled, pushing the napkin further into my pocket. "I don't know."

Her lips pursed. "Mmhmm."

I frowned. "What?"

She took a slow sip of her coffee. "Nothing." Then, with a smirk, "Just wondering if I should be picking out a bridesmaid dress or a black dress for the funeral."

I rolled my eyes. "Dramatic."

She waggled her brows. "You love me for it."

But even as I tucked it into my pocket—

Even as my fingers smoothed over the fabric like muscle memory—

It stayed with me.

Because it wasn't just words.

It was a promise.

And I wasn't sure which part of me wanted to ignore it—

And which part of me didn't.

A moment later, my phone buzzed, my heart jumping into my throat.

A message from an unknown number.

Cassian. My name is Cassian.

Kennedy

4

T he days had passed in a blur of coffee orders, clinking mugs, and the steady hum of conversation. Work had a way of swallowing time, and I let it. It was easier this way—keeping my hands busy, keeping my mind full of everything but him. But the moments in between? The quiet pauses?

That's when I felt it.

That lingering awareness. That pulse of something just beneath my skin.

I didn't want to be thinking about him. About the green-eyed stranger who walked into my life like he already belonged there. But my mind had other plans.

I hadn't told Sienna.

Not about the text.

Not about the way his name—Cassian—felt like it carried weight, like saying it out loud might make it real.

Still, there was something about the way he had looked at Cassian. Something unsettled.

Something I refused to think about.

I sighed, rubbing a hand over my tired eyes. The coffee shop had slowed to a lull, only a few stragglers lingering with their half-empty cups. Sienna was leaning against the counter, half-scrolling through her phone, half-watching me like she was waiting for me to say something.

I ignored her.

She didn't.

"Alright, spill it."

I blinked. "Spill what?"

Sienna clicked her tongue, setting her phone down. "You've been in your head all day. Your very moody, very suspicious head. And since I know it's not about Jaxon—thank God—there's only one explanation."

I arched a brow. "Oh? Enlighten me."

Her lips curved. "Green eyes. Tall. Broody. Showed up at our coffee shop like some romance novel cliché."

I huffed a laugh, shaking my head. "You need to stop reading those mafia books."

Sienna grinned. "Never." Then, after a beat, her eyes narrowed. "But you are thinking about him, aren't you?"

I didn't answer.

Because that was an answer.

And when my phone buzzed on the counter, my stomach dipped.

I glanced down.

A message.

Cassian.

My lips parted slightly, my chest tightening in that strange, unfamiliar way.

I had almost convinced myself I was imagining it. The pull. The way he seemed to linger in my thoughts when I wasn't paying attention.

But now—Now, here he was. Again.

Reaching out, like it was inevitable. Like we were inevitable.

My fingers hesitated over the screen.

This should be easy. I should ignore him.

So why was I still staring?

I exhaled, shoving my phone into my apron pocket.

Nope.

Not doing this right now.

I turned back to the espresso machine, falling into the mindless rhythm of the shop—grind, pull, steam, pour, repeat. But even as I moved through the motions, my thoughts weren't on the orders.

They were on him.

The next time I pulled my phone out, I told myself it was just to check the time.

But my eyes flicked right to his name.

Before I could stop myself, I was already untying my apron and slipping into the back room, my heart pounding just a little harder than I wanted to admit.

I leaned against the counter, staring at the message.

I could ignore it. I should ignore it.

Instead, I bit the inside of my cheek, then finally—

Cassian: *If you've been thinking about me the way I've been thinking about you. ;)*

I scoffed under my breath, shaking my head.

Me: *Bold of you to assume I even noticed your absence.*

The response came almost instantly.

Cassian: *So you did notice.*

A slow warmth unfurled in my chest.

Me: *You left an impression, alright. The jury's still out on whether it's a good one.*

I barely had time to set my phone down before it buzzed again.

Cassian: *Then let me make my case properly—Friday night. Dinner. Just you and me.*

I hesitated.

Not because I didn't know my answer.

Because I already did.

Me: *Fine. But if you bore me, I'm leaving with dessert.*

A pause.

Then—

Cassian: *You **are** the dessert.*

I stared at the screen, my pulse kicking up. Sienna's voice suddenly cut through my thoughts. "You're blushing."

I jerked my head up to see her leaning against the doorframe, arms crossed, a knowing smirk on her face.

I rolled my eyes, slipping my phone back into my pocket. "I hate you."

"You love me," she countered smoothly, pushing off the frame. "And, by the way, that was hands down the most dramatic way I've ever seen someone agree to a date."

I frowned. "What?"

Sienna gestured toward my pocket with her straw. "Babe. You read that text like it was a prophecy and then stared at it like you were waiting for it to change your life." She smirked. "Did it?"

I huffed, shaking my head. "It's not a date."

She snorted, sipping her iced coffee like she was enjoying every second of this. "Yeah, and I technically help run this shop."

"You do help run this shop," I shot back.

"Exactly. And technically, this is a date." She tilted her head with a knowing look. "You just agreed to dinner with a man who is clearly obsessed with you. At what point does it stop being 'just a meal' and start being—oh, I don't know—an affair of the heart?"

I blinked at her. "Did you just say 'affair of the heart'?"

She grinned. "It felt appropriate."

I exhaled through my nose, shaking my head. "It's just dinner."

Sienna shrugged like she didn't believe me for a second. "Sure, babe. Whatever helps you sleep at night."

I ignored her and turned back to the counter, wiping it down, pretending like my skin wasn't still buzzing from that last text.

I spent the rest of my shift pretending I wasn't aware of my phone in my pocket. I wasn't waiting for another text. I wasn't replaying our conversation in my head, picking apart every word.

Except—maybe I was.

By the time my shift ended, the sun had already dipped below the buildings, casting long shadows through the café windows. I pulled off my apron, stretched the stiffness from my shoulders, and told myself this wasn't a big deal.

It was just dinner.

Just one night.

But as I stepped outside, the brisk air brushing against my skin, my mind was already racing ahead to Friday.

And no matter how hard I tried to ignore it, a part of me knew—I was already counting down the days.

The rest of the workweek passed in a blur.

Between the usual rushes at the shop, Sienna's relentless teasing, and Jaxon's sudden radio silence, I barely had time to process what I'd agreed to.

But every time I had a quiet moment—every time my phone buzzed and his name appeared on my screen—I felt it.

That pull.

Cassian didn't text me obsessively. He didn't flood me with messages or ask pointless questions.

No.

His words were precise. Measured. Just enough to keep him in my head without trying too hard.

It was infuriating.

It was working.

So by the time Friday night rolled around, I found myself standing in front of my closet, hands on my hips, wondering when the hell I had started caring about what to wear.

It was just dinner.

And yet, my closet looked like a war zone, half the contents tossed across my bed as if some perfect outfit might magically reveal itself beneath the wreckage.

Sienna, sitting cross-legged on my bed, let out a dramatic sigh. "If you ask me one more time if you should go classy or sexy, I swear to God, I'm throwing this entire wardrobe out."

I shot her a glare over my shoulder. "I didn't ask you that."

"You were about to." She smirked.

I huffed, turning back to the disaster in front of me. "I don't understand what the big deal is, it's just dinner."

Sienna snorted. "Which is why I'm here to make sure you don't embarrass yourself."

She propped her chin in her hand, watching me like I was some kind of entertainment. "Face it, babe. This guy has you hooked."

I didn't respond.

Because denying it would be pointless.

Sienna grinned like she'd won something. "So... sexy."

I gave her a look. "I was thinking classy."

She waved a dismissive hand. "Sexy classy."

I let out a long breath, turning back to the closet.

Maybe she had a point.

It had been a long time since I'd done this. Since I cared enough to do this. I used to love getting ready for dates, back when dating was simple—back when it was fun. But now? Now it felt different. Like I had to remind myself that this wasn't anything serious.

Sienna stretched out on my bed, ankles crossed, watching as I finally settled on an outfit. I ran my fingers over the fabric, smoothing it out against my palms, feeling the soft, silky material between my fingers.

"Well?" I asked, glancing at her for approval.

Sienna tilted her head, her gaze dragging over the dress before a slow smirk curved her lips. "Sexy classy," she declared. "Told you."

I rolled my eyes but didn't argue. The dress was sleek—nothing too over-the-top, just enough to make me feel like I had actually put in some effort. A deep, wine-red color, soft against my skin, hugging in all the right places without screaming look at me. Simple. Elegant. But still... enticing.

Sienna wiggled her brows, eyes gleaming. "So, where's he taking you?"

I smoothed the fabric of my dress again, trying to sound casual. "Some Italian place downtown."

"Oh, fancy," she teased. "Rich and mysterious. The dream."

I rolled my eyes. "Maybe you should go out with him then? How many times do I have to tell you, it's just dinner!"

"Uh-huh." She smirked, clearly noticing how worked up I was—probably from nerves. "Tell that to your reflection—you've changed outfits three times."

I shot her a glare, but she just grinned.

"Whatever," I muttered, grabbing my bag. "Don't wait up."

"Text me when you get there," she said, flopping back onto my bed. "And, you know... if he turns out to be a serial killer, drop a pin."

"Noted," I deadpanned.

As I grabbed my keys, I could still hear her laughter behind me. But even as I shut the door, even as I stepped outside into the cool night air, my pulse had already picked up. I wasn't nervous. At least, that's what I told myself.

Kennedy

5

The evening breeze brushed against my skin as I stepped out of my apartment building, the distant hum of the city settling into the background. I exhaled, rolling my shoulders, trying to shake off the last bit of nerves.

It's just dinner.

The words repeated in my head as I slid into my car, gripping the steering wheel a little too tightly. I wasn't even sure why I was nervous. It wasn't like this was my first date ever. And yet, something about this—about him—felt different.

As I pulled onto the road, the quiet purr of the engine filled the space, but my mind was still tangled in the last few days.

Cassian.

The way his name had lingered in my thoughts even when I tried not to think about him. The way his messages had felt like a pull, something subtle but unshakable.

I flicked on the radio, letting the music spill into the car, grounding me.

Just dinner.

I repeated it, out loud this time, like saying it made it true.

The city stretched out before me, golden lights blurring past in soft streaks. Friday nights in the city were always the same—a steady stream of cars, restaurants packed with people laughing over wine and candlelight, couples tucked into the glow of dimly lit bars.

I tapped my fingers against the wheel, forcing my focus forward.

This wasn't a big deal.

At least, that's what I kept telling myself.

The city was alive with a low hum of energy as I pulled up to the restaurant. The soft glow of streetlights reflected off the pavement, and the buzz of conversation spilled from the entrance. It was the kind of place that exuded quiet luxury—expensive, understated, exclusive.

And yet, I couldn't shake the feeling that something felt... off.

I scanned the crowd outside, searching for Cassian. No sign of him near the entrance. My fingers curled slightly around the strap of my bag as I stepped onto the sidewalk, my heels clicking softly against the stone.

Then, I spotted him.

Not inside. Not waiting near the doors.

Cassian was leaning against a sleek, black luxury car parked just along the curb, one hand tucked into his pocket, the other holding his phone loosely at his side. He looked effortlessly composed, his sharp green eyes already locked onto mine the moment I saw him, like he'd been waiting for this exact moment.

My stomach did something I refused to acknowledge.

My breath hitched, but I smoothed it over as I approached, forcing my voice to stay even. "Should we go inside?"

Cassian pushed off the car, slipping his phone into his pocket as his lips curved—not quite a smirk, but something close. "Not tonight. Change of plans."

Before I could question him, he reached for my hand. Slow. Deliberate.

My pulse jumped as he lifted it to his lips, pressing the faintest kiss to my knuckles. The kind of kiss that wasn't rushed, wasn't casual—it was intentional.

I slowed, eyebrows lifting slightly. "Is this the part where I start to worry?"

His lips curved, shaking his head slowly. "Get in."

He reached for the door, opening it for me. A silent invitation.

I hesitated, my grip tightening slightly around my purse. "You're just… changing the location?"

Cassian leaned against the open door, watching me with something dangerously unreadable in his expression. "Do you trust me?"

A loaded question. One I didn't have an answer for.

I should have said no. I should have told him that this was ridiculous, that we already had plans. But something about the way he was looking at me—steady, like he already knew my answer—made it impossible to walk away. I exhaled sharply. Then, before I could talk myself out of it, I stepped inside.

Cassian shut the door behind me, rounding the front and sliding into the driver's seat with effortless ease. The moment he settled in, his cologne—dark, woodsy, rich—filled the space between us. The door barely clicked shut before he shifted into drive, steering us smoothly away from the curb.

For a while, neither of us spoke. The city lights blurred past, a sea of gold and blue streaking against the windows.

I exhaled slowly, trying to find my footing in the unexpected shift of plans. "Are you going to tell me where we're going, or is this part of some grand mystery?"

Cassian chuckled, shaking his head slightly as he drove. "Something tells me you like a good mystery."

I arched a brow, glancing at him. "And what makes you think I like mysteries?"

He shot me a knowing look, amusement flickering in his sharp green eyes. "You tell me, detective."

I huffed, shaking my head. He wasn't exactly wrong.

I'd always loved mystery thrillers—the kind that kept me guessing, where every twist mattered. Maybe it was because I liked knowing there was always an answer, that all the pieces would eventually fit together. Even if I didn't see it coming.

But this?

This wasn't a book. And Cassian wasn't some fictional detective case waiting to be cracked.

I should have asked him then. Pushed for answers. But instead, I found myself leaning into it, just a little.

I tilted my head, shooting him a skeptical look. "You think you have me all figured out, huh?"

Cassian glanced at me, his green eyes flicking over my face before returning to the road.

His smirk deepened, slow and deliberate. "No, Kennedy."

His voice dipped lower, softer—an amused hum beneath the words.

"But I will."

A shiver ran down my spine.

The low purr of the car's engine blended with the city sounds outside, the occasional honk or distant murmur of pedestrians passing by. Inside, though, it was quiet. Not an awkward silence—something else. Something electrifying.

I shifted slightly in my seat, smoothing my hands over my dress, feeling the silk beneath my fingertips. He drove effortlessly, one hand on the wheel, the other resting casually on the console between us.

He didn't rush. Didn't fill the silence with pointless conversation.

It should've put me at ease.

It didn't.

Because even with the quiet, even with his focus on the road, I felt him; The presence of him.

And when the next stoplight turned red, he did something that sent a shiver down my spine.

His hand, slow and deliberate, brushed against my knee.

Just for a second. Barely even a touch.

A pause.

A test.

My breath caught.

Then, just as effortlessly, he pulled back, like it never happened at all.

Like he wanted to see if I'd notice.

I swallowed hard, forcing myself to keep my gaze forward, to pretend like my pulse hadn't just skipped.

Cassian, of course, said nothing. Just shifted gears as the light turned green, driving like he hadn't just stolen the breath from my lungs.

A few minutes later, he turned onto a quieter street, slowing in front of a sleek, modern high-rise. The kind of building where the walls were probably lined with marble and the residents didn't bother checking price tags.

I turned to him, eyebrows raised, waiting for an explanation.

Instead, he opened his door and stepped out.

A second later, mine swung open too. Cassian stood there, offering his hand.

A challenge.

My fingers hovered for a moment before I finally placed my hand in his. His grip was warm, firm—but he didn't hold on for long. Just long enough.

As he led me toward the entrance, I glanced up at the towering building. "I thought we were going to dinner."

Cassian glanced at me, his green eyes gleaming beneath the city lights. "We are."

Something about the way he said it sent another shiver through me.

Then, without another word, he led me inside.

The building's lobby was sleek, modern—floor-to-ceiling windows framing the glittering skyline, polished marble stretching beneath our feet. A few people milled about, but Cassian didn't spare them a glance.

He led me straight to the elevators.

I stole a sideways look at him, my fingers tightening slightly around my bag. "So… still not telling me where we're going?"

Cassian pressed a button.

The top floor.

My stomach dipped.

He turned to me, his expression unreadable. "Patience, Kennedy."

The elevator doors slid shut, cocooning us in a hushed, intimate quiet. The city sounds faded, replaced only by the soft whir of ascent.

I shifted slightly, glancing at the mirrored walls. "You know, you have a bad habit of being cryptic."

Cassian chuckled under his breath, shifting slightly to face me. "And you have a bad habit of overthinking."

I scoffed. "I do not."

His gaze flickered over me, slow and deliberate, before settling on my eyes. "No?"

I held his stare, refusing to be the first to look away.

The air between us felt heavier.

Then—a brush of warmth.

A hand at the small of my back.

Light. Steady. Just enough to guide me forward as the elevator doors closed.

I swallowed, shifting slightly—but Cassian didn't move his hand right away. He let it linger for a moment longer than necessary.

Long enough for my body to register it.

Long enough for me to wonder if it was intentional.

I exhaled through my nose, crossing my arms to keep from fidgeting.

Cassian smirked, like he knew.

Then—ding.

I turned, expecting a lavish penthouse.

Instead, the elevator doors slid open to a rooftop.

I blinked, stepping forward instinctively as a cool breeze wrapped around me, carrying the distant hum of the city below.

Not a penthouse.

A rooftop.

Cassian stepped beside me, hands slipping casually into his pockets as he watched me take it in.

Soft, golden lights traced the edges of the space, casting a warm glow against the sleek outdoor dining set before us. A table set for two stood near the railing, framed by the glittering skyline. Silver-domed trays rested on fine china, waiting to be uncovered.

The way the night air wrapped around us, crisp and cool, carrying the distant hum of the city below.

I blinked. "This is… not a restaurant."

Cassian smirked, stepping ahead, his hands casually sliding into his pockets. "No. It's not."

I turned to him, brows raised, waiting for an explanation.

Instead, he simply nodded toward the table. "Come on."

I hesitated.

This was his place.

Not just some rooftop. His penthouse rooftop.

The realization settled in my chest, pressing against something uncertain.

Cassian watched me, amusement flickering behind his green eyes. "You don't trust me."

It wasn't a question.

I exhaled slowly, meeting his gaze head-on. "I don't know you."

Something shifted in his expression—just for a second.

Then, he extended his hand, palm up, waiting.

Another invitation.

Another challenge.

I hesitated for half a heartbeat. Then, finally, I stepped forward, slipping my fingers into his.

Warm. Steady. Sure.

His lips twitched—satisfied.

And just like that, he led me toward the table, the city glowing behind us. I hesitated as he pulled out my chair, his movements fluid, unrushed. Everything about this felt intentional—too carefully crafted to be anything but deliberate.

Cassian waited, watching me with that same quiet patience, his hand resting lightly on the back of the chair.

A silent dare.

I exhaled, smoothing my dress before lowering myself into the seat. The cushion was plush beneath me, the cool night air carrying the faintest hint of crisp wine and something richer—something distinctly him.

Cassian took the seat across from me, his movements seamless. The flickering candlelight danced across his features, casting sharp shadows over his cheekbones, the slight curve of his lips.

I glanced at the spread before us—two pristine plates, a bottle of wine already uncorked, delicate silver trays concealing whatever meal he had planned. It wasn't just a dinner; it was an experience. Every detail, from the glowing skyline framing us to the elegance of the table setting, felt calculated.

Finally, I broke the silence. "So, what—you just happen to keep a private rooftop dinner setup on standby?"

Cassian's mouth twitched. "Something like that."

I scoffed, picking up my napkin and draping it over my lap. "Right. Because that's completely normal."

His gaze remained steady, amused. "Normal is relative."

I huffed a quiet laugh, shaking my head. "You do realize this is a little much for a first date, right?"

Cassian reached for the bottle of wine, fingers wrapping around the neck as he poured a deep, crimson stream into my glass. "And yet, you're here."

I opened my mouth, but no argument came to mind.

Because he was right.

I was here.

And despite myself, I was intrigued.

Cassian poured his wine before leaning back, his fingers curling loosely around the stem. "Do you always question everything, Kennedy?"

I lifted a brow. "Do you always expect people to just go along with whatever this is?"

Cassian smirked, his green eyes gleaming. "I don't expect anything. But I do like seeing how people react."

He tilted his head slightly. "And you, detective, are very fun to watch."

A slow, simmering warmth spread through my chest. I reached for my wine, taking a sip just to keep myself occupied. The taste was smooth, velvety, with a hint of something dark lingering at the back of my tongue.

Cassian's gaze never wavered.

I set my glass down, trying not to acknowledge the way my pulse had picked up. "So, are you going to tell me what's under those trays, or do I have to play along with your whole 'mysterious stranger' act?"

Cassian exhaled a chuckle, reaching for the silver dome over his plate. "Since you're so impatient."

With a flick of his wrist, he lifted the tray.

I blinked.

Pasta. Rich, golden strands coated in a silky sauce, flecks of fresh herbs scattered across the dish. It was simple. Classic. The kind of meal that didn't need extravagance to be good.

Something about that struck me as unexpected.

Cassian gestured lazily toward my plate. "Go on."

I hesitated before reaching for my tray, lifting the cover to reveal the same dish. The scent of garlic, parmesan, and fresh basil curled into the cool air, making my stomach tighten.

I glanced at him. "You really like the theatrics, huh?"

Cassian leaned forward slightly, resting an elbow on the table. "I like making an impression."

I rolled my eyes, twirling a forkful of pasta. "Well, mission accomplished."

His gaze flicked down to my mouth as I took a bite.

I swallowed.

His lips parted slightly, the amusement in his eyes darkening by just a fraction. "Good?"

I lifted a shoulder. "Not bad."

Cassian hummed, taking a slow sip of his wine. "I'll take it."

I exhaled, shaking my head. "Okay, now your turn."

Cassian arched a brow. "For what?"

"For me to figure you out." I tilted my head, studying him. "You like to be in control. You're too smooth for this to be the first time you've done something like this."

His expression remained unreadable, his only response was a slow sip of wine.

I narrowed my eyes. "You're rich."

His lips quirked. "Clearly."

I set my fork down, resting my chin in my hand. "And you like keeping people on their toes."

Cassian smirked. "Is that so?"

"You tell me." I held his gaze. "You brought me here instead of a restaurant. You dodge direct answers. And you love watching people's reactions." I let my eyes flick over him, taking him in the way I had at the coffee shop. "You like power."

Cassian didn't move. Didn't blink.

But something shifted. Just barely.

Then, he leaned forward, resting his forearms on the table. "Very good, detective,"

I blinked.

Cassian smirked, picking up his fork. "But you missed something."

I swallowed, suddenly hyper-aware of the distance between us.

"And what's that?" I asked, my voice quieter.

Cassian twirled his pasta, lifting a bite to his mouth before answering.

He chewed, slow and deliberate, watching me the entire time. Then, after swallowing, he leaned in just slightly, elbows resting against the table.

"You think I like power," he mused, voice smooth, considering. "That I enjoy control."

His green eyes glinted under the soft rooftop lights. "But that's not quite it."

I tilted my head. "Oh? Then what is it?"

Cassian's gaze flickered over me, assessing, thoughtful. Then, he smirked.

"I don't care about power," he said simply. "I care about knowing what people want."

I blinked, caught off guard by the answer.

Cassian swirled the wine in his glass, watching the deep red liquid coat the sides.

"Everyone wants something, Kennedy. Some people just don't know what yet." His gaze lifted, locking onto mine. "I like figuring it out."

A strange, nervous energy curled in my stomach.

I exhaled through my nose, gripping my fork. "Wow," I muttered. "That's not ominous at all."

Cassian chuckled, setting his glass down. "You asked."

I narrowed my eyes at him. "And you love when people do."

He lifted his glass toward me, a slow, lazy movement.

"To curiosity," he murmured.

I hesitated, then tapped my glass against his.

"To mystery," I countered.

Cassian's smirk deepened. "And to the ones who can't resist chasing it."

I took a sip of wine, but I wasn't sure I tasted it.

Because for the first time, I wasn't entirely sure who was figuring who out.

Cassian let out a quiet laugh, but he picked up his fork, twirling the pasta with a casual ease. And yet—even as I turned my focus back to my plate—I could still feel him watching me.

Cassian twirled his fork slowly, lifting a bite to his mouth, his movements unrushed.

Deliberate.

I mirrored him, stabbing my fork into my plate and taking a small bite, my stomach flipping when I realized he was still watching me.

He ate like he did everything else—calm, composed, as if nothing in the world could rattle him.

The space between us felt different now. Not heavy. Not awkward. Just… charged.

Somewhere in the background, a soft melody floated through hidden speakers—low, instrumental, something smooth and easy, like jazz or an old love song. It filled the quiet, weaving into the clink of silverware and the distant hum of the city below.

It was almost like we were testing each other—who would look away first, who would fold under the quiet weight of this moment.

I lifted my wine glass, taking a slow sip, feeling the warmth settle in my chest. Cassian smirked faintly, mirroring me, his green eyes sharp, amused. Like he knew exactly what he was doing.

The seconds stretched.

I set my glass down, tilting my head slightly. "Do you always stare this much?"

Cassian leaned back, eyes never leaving mine. "Only when I like what I'm looking at."

A flicker of heat rolled through me. I rolled my lips together, suppressing a smile. "That line was awful."

Cassian exhaled a chuckle, setting his glass down. "And yet, you haven't looked away."

Ugh. Shut up.

The silence wasn't uncomfortable. It wasn't forced. It just… was.

And maybe that was the most unsettling part.

The music swelled slightly, the notes deep and slow.

After a long moment, Cassian placed his napkin beside his plate and stood.

I blinked, looking up at him. "What are you doing?"

Cassian extended his hand. "Dance with me."

My stomach flipped. "Here?"

One side of his mouth lifted. "I don't see anyone stopping us."

I hesitated. But only for a second.

Then, before I could overthink it, I reached for his hand.

Cassian's fingers curled around mine, warm and steady, as he guided me to my feet. I swallowed, my pulse skipping ahead of me.

He didn't pull me in right away. Just kept hold of my hand, thumb brushing along the inside of my wrist—slow, deliberate.

The music swayed through the air, soft and intoxicating, wrapping around us like silk.

Cassian's other hand came to rest just above my waist, fingers pressing lightly against the fabric of my dress.

I placed my free hand against his shoulder, feeling the solid warmth of him through his suit.

We moved slowly, not perfectly, not practiced, but effortlessly in sync.

Cassian wasn't leading with exaggerated movements, wasn't trying to impress me. It wasn't about that.

It was the closeness.

The quiet between words.

The way his fingers flexed ever so slightly against my waist when I stepped in just a little closer.

I exhaled through my nose, tilting my head slightly to glance up at him. "Do you do this often?"

Cassian's lips quirked, amusement flickering in his gaze. "What? Dance?"

"This. The whole… mystery act."

His fingers skimmed the small of my back as he turned us slightly, our steps easy, unhurried. "And what makes you think it's an act?"

I narrowed my eyes at him, but my lips twitched. "Because nobody is this smooth naturally."

Cassian let out a low chuckle, the sound rolling through me.

He didn't argue.

Instead, he shifted just slightly, closing the last inch of space between us.

Heat licked up my spine, my breath catching in my throat.

The city stretched out around us—glittering lights reflecting off the glass railing, the world feeling somehow smaller, quieter up here.

And Cassian?

Cassian was watching me like he had all the time in the world.

I wet my lips. "So?"

He arched a brow. "So?"

"Is this where you tell me you never do this?" I challenged, my voice softer now.

Cassian hummed, considering.

Then, with that same unreadable smirk, he murmured—"No, Kennedy. This is where I tell you I've been waiting to."

My stomach flipped.

Before I could process it—before I could say anything—Cassian's hand slid higher up my back, his thumb grazing my spine. His other hand, the one still holding mine, loosened just slightly before pulling me in.

And then—His lips brushed against my jaw.

A featherlight touch.

A test.

My breath hitched.

My fingers curled against his shoulder, nails lightly dragging against the fabric.

Cassian stilled, waiting.

Giving me a choice.

I didn't think. Didn't hesitate.

I turned my head ever so slightly—just enough.

And then his lips were on mine.

Soft at first.

Testing.

Then, when I didn't pull away—when I tilted further into him—it deepened.

Cassian's fingers pressed firmer into my back, pulling me flush against him. The music, the city, the rooftop—it all melted into the background.

All I could feel was the warmth of him, the steady control in the way he kissed me. Like he knew exactly what he was doing.

Like he'd wanted this.

Like he'd known I would want it, too.

I exhaled softly against his lips, and I felt the curve of his smirk before he pulled back, just enough to make me chase the space between us.

I swallowed, my pulse thrumming.

Cassian's gaze flickered over my face, his amusement cooling into something deeper. Something unreadable.

His fingers brushed against my spine, barely there.

I swallowed. "Is this the part where I ask what you want?" My voice was softer now, my own words betraying me.

Cassian tilted his head slightly, a quiet hum slipping past his lips. "No, Kennedy."

His thumb traced the inside of my wrist. "This is the part where I wait for you to figure it out."

My stomach flipped.

The weight of his words settled between us, heady and thick.

I didn't move. Neither did he.

Not yet.

But something told me—I wouldn't be waiting long.

The cool evening air curled around us, but I still felt the warmth of his touch, the slow burn where his lips had been. My breath was steady, but my pulse betrayed me—a quiet thrum of something I wasn't ready to name.

Cassian studied me, his gaze unreadable yet heavy with knowing. Like he was waiting for something.

Like he could feel it, too.

The song still played softly in the background, but neither of us moved to dance again. The moment had already happened—lingering in the space between us, unspoken but undeniable.

I exhaled, wetting my lips. "That was…"

Cassian's head tilted slightly, lips twitching in amusement. "Unexpected?"

I huffed a soft laugh. "I was going to say—bold."

His smirk deepened, effortlessly. "You say that like you didn't want it."

A slow heat curled in my stomach.

I could lie. Play coy. Pretend this was something casual, something easy to walk away from.

But when I met his gaze, steady and assured, I knew better.

Cassian knew better, too.

I swallowed, my voice quieter now. "And what if I did?"

Cassian hummed, considering. Then, after a beat, he murmured, "Then, we might both be in trouble."

A slow heat unfurled in my chest.

He didn't move closer, didn't press—but I felt the pull just the same. That quiet, magnetic something was drawing me toward him. The same thing that had been there from the moment I first saw him.

I rolled my lips together, my fingers twitching slightly at my sides.

I could stay here.

Just a little longer.

As if reading my thoughts, Cassian's voice dipped, smooth as silk. "Come inside."

A simple invitation.

But his tone—low, deliberate, laced with something deeper—made my stomach tighten.

My eyes flicked toward the penthouse, then back to him.

My pulse quickened.

Not from fear. From anticipation.

I wasn't stupid. I knew exactly what this was.

And yet—I was still standing here.

Still looking at him.

Still considering it.

I inhaled slowly, heart hammering against my ribs as I made my choice.

And when I finally stepped forward—when I let him take my hand, his fingers curling lightly around mine—Cassian's smirk turned into something softer.

Something far more dangerous.

Because we both knew—this was only the beginning.

Kennedy

6

Cassian had led me through the entryway, the soft click of the door shutting behind us sealing me into his world. The air inside was warm, rich with something familiar—him. A scent I had begun to recognize even when he wasn't near.

His penthouse wasn't exactly what I had expected. Sure, it was sleek, modern, all glass and dark wood and expensive lighting. But it wasn't cold. There were books stacked haphazardly on the coffee table, a half-empty glass sat near the couch, and a leather jacket lay draped lazily over the armrest. Lived-in.

Cassian walked ahead, loosening his tie, his eyes flicking to mine like he was waiting for a reaction.

I raised a brow, glancing around. "This is way less villainous than I expected."

Cassian smirked, heading toward a sleek bar cart near the windows. "Should I be concerned that you expected a lair?"

I shrugged, toeing off my heels. "I don't know. I pictured something a little more… dramatic. A fireplace. Maybe a glass case with a rare artifact you stole from an auction."

Cassian let out a chuckle, reaching for a bottle. The sound of liquid sloshed into crystal before he grabbed two glasses, setting them on the counter with an effortless clink.

Then, without looking up, he said— "Tequila, right?"

My stomach dipped. "Oh, you remembered?"

He slid one of the glasses toward me.

A perfectly made Tequila Sunrise.

I blinked.

The layers of deep red and gold swirled together under the kitchen lights, a slow, lazy mix of sunset hues. I ran my thumb along the glass before lifting it to my lips, the familiar tang of citrus and tequila brushing my tongue.

Cassian leaned against the counter, watching me with a knowing smirk. "You strike me as a girl who knows what she likes."

I swallowed, setting the glass down. "And you strike me as someone who likes proving a point."

I tilted my head, the smile fading just slightly. "You know, you still haven't told me what you actually do."

He met my eyes, and something in his expression shifted—barely. "You wouldn't believe me if I told you."

"Try me."

Cassian's smirk returned, smooth and practiced, before he reached for his glass again. "When in doubt—lime and salt."

I blinked, realizing he'd redirected—just like that. "That was bold of you."

Cassian clinked his glass against mine before taking a slow sip, eyes never leaving mine.

The drinks kept flowing.

One turned into two. Then three. Then, a ridiculous conversation about whether or not Cassian had ever danced to an embarrassing song in his life.

"You're telling me," I said, tipping my head back against the couch, "you've never, not once, done a dumb little two-step to a song you secretly love?"

Cassian exhaled through his nose, swirling the tequila in his glass. "Not in the way you're imagining."

I gasped, dramatically. "Not even as a kid?"

He smirked. "I wasn't exactly the 'dance around my bedroom' type."

I squinted at him. "That's... actually tragic."

Cassian's lips twitched. "Not all of us grew up choreographing dance routines in the mirror, detective."

I scoffed, setting my glass down. "Excuse you. I was a professional."

He raised a brow. "Oh?"

I grinned, standing on unsteady feet, swaying slightly. The tequila had settled warm in my bloodstream, a heady, buzzing kind of lightness. "Give me a song."

Cassian crossed his arms, watching me with lazy amusement. "You're serious?"

"Deadly."

A beat of silence.

Then, he pulled his phone from his pocket, tapped a few buttons, and suddenly—

A song filled the penthouse.

Not classical.

Not jazz.

But...

I gasped. "Is this—"

Cassian smirked, taking a slow sip of his drink.

It was.

"Mambo No. 5."

"Oh, you asshole," I muttered, already laughing as I swayed my hips, doing the absolute dumbest little dance I could think of.

Cassian just watched, thoroughly entertained.

I pointed at him, still moving. "Your turn."

He raised his glass lazily. "I think you've got this covered."

I rolled my eyes. "Come on. I know you can dance."

His smirk deepened. "I can. Doesn't mean I'm going to."

I narrowed my eyes. "Why not?"

A glint of something dangerous flickered in his expression.

"Not unless it's worth it," he murmured.

The air shifted.

Then, before I could think twice, I whispered—

"Am I worth it?"

My stomach fell to the floor.

My feet slowed, the song still playing, but neither of us were laughing anymore.

Because suddenly, I wasn't thinking about dancing. I was thinking about the way he was looking at me.

Like maybe, just maybe—this was worth it.

I took a slow step forward.

Cassian didn't move. Didn't blink.

I was still grinning, still tipsy, still reckless in the way alcohol made people brave.

And yet, when I placed my hands on his chest, his body went still.

Like he was waiting for something.

Like he was waiting for me.

I moved closer. He didn't stop me.

A slow inhale. A flicker of something dark in his eyes.

I kissed him first.

Soft.

Then—he responded.

Cassian's hand slid up my back, fingers threading into my hair as he pulled me deeper, the kiss shifting from playful to desperate in seconds.

My body reacted, pressing into his. His lips parted against mine, breath mixing with mine, his other hand gripping my waist like he was grounding himself.

I barely registered when he lifted me. Not onto the counter. Not anywhere calculated.

Just—closer.

Then, his hands wandered.

Too far. Too fast.

I tensed.

Cassian stopped immediately.

His forehead rested against mine, breath ragged, chest rising and falling as he held himself back.

A beat of silence.

Then, his hands slid to safer places. My waist. My arms.

He exhaled through his nose. "Not yet."

I swallowed. Nodded.

No pressure. No frustration. Just control.

Cassian ran his thumb over my wrist, grounding. "Come on," he murmured. "I think we've reached the limit of your tequila tolerance."

I opened my mouth to argue.

Then, I swayed.

Cassian's smug grin was the last thing I saw before my stomach turned.

The moment my stomach lurched, I barely had time to push off of him before I was scrambling to my feet, bolting toward the nearest bathroom.

Cassian was right behind me.

I barely made it before I was gripping the porcelain, my body betraying me in the worst way possible.

Of all the times to throw up.

Of all the places.

In his penthouse.

I groaned between heaves, absolutely mortified.

Cassian crouched beside me, his hand brushing the hair from my face, gathering it in one hand while the other ran slow, soothing circles down my back. He didn't speak, didn't tease. Just let me suffer in peace.

When I finally sagged back against the cool tile, eyes squeezed shut, I felt the press of a cold water bottle against my lips.

"Drink," he murmured.

I did, taking slow, cautious sips.

The worst of the nausea was fading, but the embarrassment? Still going strong.

I muttered, "I hate you."

Cassian chuckled, the sound deep and effortless. "I'm sure my bathroom feels the same way about you ."

I cracked an eye open just enough to glare. "I hope I clogged your toilet."

Cassian smirked, setting the water down before reaching for something from a nearby drawer. I barely noticed, still wallowing in my misery, until I felt the soft brush of fabric against my arm.

I blinked down at the oversized T-shirt in his hands, then up at him.

He wasn't tossing it at me—he was holding it out, patiently waiting.

"Your dress," he murmured, gaze flicking over the ruined fabric. "Didn't make it."

His lips twitched, like he was biting back a smirk. "Tragic loss, really. But I promise the dry cleaners in this building are miracle workers."

I groaned, pressing my forehead against my knee. "This is the worst night of my life."

Cassian let out a low chuckle, crouching in front of me. "That bad, huh?" His voice was smoother now, quieter. Less smug. More something else.

I peeked up at him, the teasing glint still there, but softer this time.

"You'll feel better once you change," he said, tapping the shirt lightly against my knee before holding it out again. "Unless you'd rather sleep in that."

I did not want to sleep in this tequila-soaked disaster of a dress.

I huffed, taking the shirt from his hands. His fingers brushed against mine, warm, steady.

Cassian didn't move right away. Just lingered, his gaze flicking over me—not in the way that made my stomach flip, but in the way that told me he was still watching, still making sure I was okay.

Then, with a quiet exhale, he pushed to his feet. "I'll give you a minute."

No smug comments. No unnecessary theatrics.

Just that same careful patience as he turned his back and left the room.

I exhaled slowly, fingers curling around the hem of the T-shirt before slipping it over my head. The fabric was soft, worn in a way that made it feel lived-in, and it carried the faintest trace of him—clean, woodsy, something undeniably Cassian.

By the time I peeled off my ruined dress and tugged the shirt into place, exhaustion had settled deep in my bones. The night had finally caught up with me, leaving my body heavy and my mind hazy.

I shuffled forward, my balance still slightly unsteady. Cassian was already waiting by the doorway, arms crossed as he leaned against the frame, watching me with quiet amusement.

"Alright, lightweight." His voice was softer now, something unreadable flickering behind his eyes. "Let's get you to bed."

I blinked up at him, my limbs suddenly too heavy, my skin too warm. The tequila haze was thick now, wrapping around me like a weighted blanket.

"I can take the couch," I mumbled, already half-asleep, fingers weakly gripping the hem of the oversized shirt.

Cassian's lips twitched. "Cute."

I frowned, sluggishly lifting my head to glare at him. "I mean it."

He crouched beside me, close enough that I could smell the lingering hint of his cologne—dark, woodsy, something rich and familiar.

"I know," he said, voice softer now. "But you're not."

Before I could argue, his arms slid beneath me, one under my knees, the other bracing my back.

My breath hitched.

"Cassian—"

"Relax, detective," he murmured, standing effortlessly with me in his arms. "I'll behave."

My head tipped against his shoulder, my body too exhausted to fight it.

He carried me like I weighed nothing, like it wasn't even a question.

My fingers curled into the soft fabric of his shirt, the warmth of him making my eyelids grow heavier.

"Still hate you," I muttered, words barely above a whisper.

Cassian let out a low chuckle, the sound vibrating through me. "I'll survive."

I melted into his arms as he carried me into his bedroom, taking in his muscles and warmth. I practically pouted when I felt him lay me down.

The blankets were soft, the pillows even softer. Somewhere in the distance, I heard Cassian move around the room, turning off the light, grabbing something. But I was already half-asleep, barely registering when the bed dipped slightly beside me.

He hovered over me as he sat beside me on the bed, a thumb brushing my flushed cheeks. "See you in the morning, detective."

A low hum left my lips before I could stop it.

"Stay."

Cassian stilled.

I cracked an eye open, catching the flicker of hesitation in his expression. His knuckles brushed over my temple, smoothing a stray curl behind my ear. "Careful, detective. That almost sounded like a confession."

I cracked an eye open, just enough to see him watching me.

"Shut up," I slurred. "Lie down."

Something flickered in his expression.

I curled deeper into the pillow, half-lucid, the room still tilting at an odd angle. The tequila had finally won.

Cassian tucked the blankets around me, moving with the same careful precision he always did, but this time, it wasn't calculated. It was soft.

Giving in to my request, I felt the bed dip slightly as he lay next to me.

I shifted, pressing my forehead lightly against his shoulder, half-dreaming, half-drunk. "You're warm."

Cassian's voice was low, amused. "You're hogging my bed, detective."

I smirked against the pillow, words slurred. "And I don't feel bad about it."

His low chuckle was the last thing I heard before sleep took me under.

His warmth sank in beside me, solid and steady. He didn't pull me in, didn't test the limits of what I wanted. Just laid there, his fingers absently tracing slow, thoughtless circles against the fabric of his pillow.

I didn't stir when he shifted. Didn't notice the way his fingers skimmed absently against my wrist, as if memorizing the shape of it. Didn't feel when his breaths slowed, matching mine.

I only knew that when I woke, the space beside me was empty.

I shifted, stretching my legs beneath the blankets, my body sinking into the plush mattress.

It's comfortable, almost too comfortable. The kind of comfortable that makes it easy to forget where I am, easy to forget—

Then it hit me.

The rooftop. The dancing. The kiss.

His hands were on my waist.

The way he stopped himself. Not yet.

The way I asked him to stay.

My stomach twists.

Because I don't know what's worse—the fact that I asked, or the fact that he actually did.

I turned, reaching across the bed, half-expecting to find him still there.

But I don't.

The sheets were cool where he should've been.

I groaned, rubbing my hands over my face, my head pounding in protest. I barely even made it upright before I heard the angry buzz of my phone from somewhere in the room.

I blinked against the light, squinting at the bedside table.

My phone was face down, screen lighting up with notification after notification.

I grabbed it, barely able to focus before the texts came into view.

Sienna: *Babe.*

Sienna: *Where are you???*

Sienna: *If you're dead in a ditch somewhere, I swear to God Kennedy, I will kill you myself.*

Sienna: *I'M ABOUT TO FILE A MISSING PERSONS REPORT.*

Sienna: *Jaxon is being a pain in my ass, btw. Surprise surprise.*

I groaned, running a hand through my tangled hair.

Me: *Alive. Hungover. Calm down.*

The typing bubbles appeared immediately.

Sienna: *Hungover?? BITCH.*

Sienna: *Are you still with him?*

I hesitate.

Me: *…Yes.*

Sienna: *SAY LESS. I NEED DETAILS.*

Me: *Later.*

Sienna: *Ugh. Fine. But if you disappear again, I'm putting out a statewide alert.*

I rolled my eyes, tossing my phone onto the bed with a sigh.

Just when I was about to fall back into the pillows, I heard a faint sound of movement coming from the other room.

Cassian.

I pushed myself out of bed, swaying slightly as the remnants of tequila still weighed heavily in my limbs. I glanced down, running my fingers along the hem of the oversized T-shirt, realizing just how much of him I still smell.

The hardwood was cool beneath my feet as I made my way down the hall, drawn by the familiar scent of coffee and something warm.

Cassian was at the counter, back turned, pouring two cups of coffee like this was routine.

Like this was normal.

Like I'm just supposed to be here.

Still rocking last night's dress shirt, sleeves rolled up, his tie long gone, a few buttons undone—just enough to make my stomach tighten.

He didn't look hungover. He didn't even look ruffled.

Meanwhile, I probably looked like I crawled through hell.

I barely had time to process that thought before his gaze lifted, locking onto me.

His eyes flicked down, taking in bare legs, messy hair, and the way his shirt hung off my shoulder.

The corner of his mouth twitched. "Morning, detective."

I grumbled something incoherent, padding toward the counter as he slid a coffee cup toward me.

I glanced down.

Black. No sugar.

He remembered.

I lifted the cup, taking a slow sip.

Cassian leaned against the counter, watching me, his smirk lazy.

"How's your head?"

I groaned, rubbing my temple. "Not great."

Cassian hummed, smug. "Lightweight."

"I hate you."

His smirk deepened. "I know."

I took another slow sip of coffee, letting the warmth settle the nausea still lingering in my stomach. It offered a soothing comfort, but it didn't fix the fact that I felt like a walking disaster.

Cassian didn't say anything else—just watched, that damn knowing expression never leaving his face. I shifted in my seat, suddenly very aware of the oversized T-shirt swallowing me whole, the fact that my dress was nowhere in sight.

I frowned, glancing around. "Where's my dress?"

Cassian didn't answer immediately. Instead, he set a neatly folded pile of clothes on the counter between us.

"Didn't think you'd want to wear last night's dress home."

A scoff escaped my lips. "You knew I was going to spend the night?."

Cassian smirked, slow and deliberate. "Not exactly. But considering the odds of you ruining your dress were pretty high, I had something sent up."

I narrowed my eyes. "So you planned for me to make a fool of myself?"

He tilted his head, amusement flickering behind his eyes. "No, detective. I planned for the possibility that you'd need a change of clothes. Turns out, I was right."

I groaned, rubbing my temples. "I hate that you always have an answer for everything."

His smirk deepened. "I know."

I rolled my eyes but took the clothes anyway, disappearing down the hall to change.

By the time I returned, Cassian was exactly where I left him—leaning against the counter, scrolling through his phone like he had all the time in the world.

I hesitated for a second, fingers curling around the hem of the borrowed sweater he gave me. It was soft, worn in, and smelled faintly like him—clean, woodsy, with something dark beneath it.

I cleared my throat. "I should probably get going. Sienna is already threatening to burn the café down if I don't show up soon."

Cassian finally glanced up, lips twitching. "Sounds like a real liability."

"Oh, absolutely." I sighed dramatically, grabbing my bag. "But she works for cheap."

Cassian chuckled, shaking his head as he pushed off the counter. "Come on, then. I'll take you to your car before your café turns into a crime scene."

I hesitated. "You don't have to drive me. I can just call a—"

He arched a brow, already heading toward the door. "Do I look like the kind of guy who lets a woman Uber home after spending the night in his bed?"

My stomach did something it really shouldn't have at the sound of that.

I schooled my expression, rolling my eyes. "God forbid I damage your chivalrous reputation."

Cassian just smirked, opening the door. "Let's go, detective."

And just like that, I followed him outside.

The air was crisp, the lingering chill of early morning wrapped around me as we stepped onto the quiet street. Cassian unlocked the car with a lazy flick of his wrist, the sleek black vehicle humming to life.

I slid into the passenger seat, the door shut with a quiet thunk. The scent inside was familiar —distinctly his.

The drive was quiet at first, the city still waking up, streets glowing gold with early morning light.

I fidgeted with the hem of my borrowed sweater, the fabric soft against my fingers, feeling strange about leaving.

Cassian's voice cut through the silence.

"You don't have to look so miserable."

I scowled, arms crossed over my chest. "I'm not miserable."

His smirk was lazily amused. "You're pouting."

"I am not—"

Cassian just hummed, like he didn't believe me.

The silence stretched again, thick with something unspoken.

When we finally pulled up beside my car, a new kind of tension settled between us.

Cassian didn't unlock the doors right away.

Instead, he shifted slightly, his arm draped along the back of my seat, head tilted just enough to face me. The early morning glow casted him in softer shadows, his green eyes sharper in the quiet light.

I drummed my fingers lightly against my thigh, rolling my lips together. "This is the part where you say you'll call me."

His lips twitched. "Would you answer?"

I exhaled through my nose, gaze flicking toward the windshield. "Probably not."

Cassian hummed, like he already knew the answer. "At least you're honest."

A small smile tugged at my lips, but it didn't last—not when the moment stretched between us, thick and heavy, something neither of us were addressing.

I felt his eyes on me.

Watching. Waiting.

My fingers curled around the strap of my bag. "So… Do I at least get a five-star rating as a houseguest?"

Cassian huffed a quiet laugh, the corner of his mouth twitched. "You drool in your sleep."

I gasped. "I do not."

His smirk deepened. "You want me to prove it?"

I scowled, smacking his arm lightly before reaching for the door handle, willing my face to cool. But before I could move—

His fingers brushed my jaw.

A stray strand of hair tucked behind my ear.

My breath stuttered.

His hand lingered, warm against my skin.

"Are you always this much trouble?" he murmured, voice low.

I smirk, despite the heat curling in my stomach. "Not even a little."

Cassian hummed, fingers tracing my jaw like he was memorizing it. His smirk didn't fade—but something shifted. Darkened.

"Liar."

I shifted slightly, fingers wrapping around the door handle, trying to remember how to breathe.

Cassian's gaze flickered over me, something unreadable simmering in his expression. "You'll see me again."

I swallowed, fingers curling around the handle of the door. That shouldn't have made my stomach flip. But it did.

I nodded, exhaling slowly. "I know."

I didn't wait for a response. I pushed the door open and stepped out, my heart hammering against my ribs, the cool morning air brushing against my skin like a warning—like a reminder that whatever this was, it shouldn't feel like that.

Like something I wasn't ready to leave.

Once I made it to my car, I reached for the driver's side handle—

Footsteps. Fast. Certain.

Before I could react, a hand wrapped around my wrist, firm but not forceful.

A pause. A warning. A choice.

I barely had time to turn before he was there, standing in front of me, too close, his grip steady, his gaze flicking between my lips and my eyes like he was fighting some invisible war.

A war he was about to lose.

Cassian exhaled slowly.

Then—he kissed me.

Not rushed. Not careful.

It was a slow, deliberate kind of possession. A claim.

His lips pressed against mine, firm, coaxing, like he knew exactly how to unravel me one touch at a time.

I took in a breath, but the second my lips parted, he was there—tasting, taking, deepening.

His hand slid from my wrist to my jaw, fingers brushing over my throat, tilting my head just enough to pull me further into him. His other hand found my waist, fingers pressing, curling, gripping.

Like he couldn't help himself.

Like he didn't want to.

I let out a quiet, shuddering breath against his mouth, and Cassian responded instantly.

A quiet sound rumbled in his chest, his grip tightening as his lips slanted over mine again, rougher this time, hungrier.

The kind of kiss that erases everything else.

The kind of kiss that makes you forget why you ever thought leaving was a good idea.

I shouldn't have.

I shouldn't have sunk into him. I shouldn't have gripped onto his shirt, pulling him closer, tilting my chin so he could kiss me deeper.

And yet—

My nails grazed his jaw, his stubble rough against my fingertips, against my mouth.

Cassian made a quiet sound—a curse, a growl, something primal and low—before his teeth grazed my bottom lip. A light bite. A warning.

I inhaled sharply.

I felt him smirk against my lips, like he liked my response. Like he wanted more of it.

He moved closer, pressing me against the side of my car. His fingers trailed down my spine, dragging fire in their wake.

A delicious, dizzying heat coiled low in my stomach.

I don't know who pulled away first.

Maybe it was him.

Maybe it was me.

All I know is when his lips finally parted from mine, I gasped.

Not from exertion. Not from shock.

From wanting more.

Cassian stayed close, his forehead resting against mine, his breath warm, uneven.

His thumb traced the corner of my lips, like he was memorizing them.

Like he already knew he was going to kiss me again.

"Now you can go," he murmured, voice rough, ragged.

A challenge. A dare.

I exhaled sharply, my fingers still curled into his shirt.

He stepped back.

The cool air rushed between us like a cruel reminder of reality.

I watched as he turned, walking back to his car, his movements were too calm, too controlled, too Cassian.

But I didn't move.

Not yet.

Because my body was still humming.

Because my lips were still tingling.

Because I wasn't sure I was ready to let him go just yet.

Kennedy

7

I stepped inside and shut the door behind me, the weight of the night finally catching up.

The TV was still on—some nature documentary playing on low volume for Luna, who blinked at me from the armrest like I'd just disturbed her peace. Her tail flicked once in lazy judgment.

"Hello to you, too," I muttered, kicking off my shoes and dropping my bag by the door.

She stretched out dramatically, then meowed—loud and unapologetic.

"Alright, alright," I said, making a beeline to the kitchen. "I know, you're starving. Over here knocking on death's door."

I laughed, pulling open the cabinet where I kept her food, grabbed a can, and popped it open. The second she heard it, Luna trotted in with all the arrogance of a creature who believed she owned the place. I scooped the food into her bowl and gave it a little stir with the spoon—because apparently, she wouldn't touch it unless it was "fluffed."

Once she was satisfied and munching away, I leaned against the counter, rubbing my eyes. My body felt like it had been wrung out—exhausted and light all at once.

My phone buzzed on the counter.

Sienna.

Sienna: *So??? Alive?? Or abducted by Tequila Man??*

I smiled, thumbs already moving.

Me: *Alive. Close early.*

The dots appeared immediately.

Sienna: *I'm bringing caffeine. You bring the tea.*

I huffed a quiet laugh and tossed the phone onto the couch before grabbing a glass of water and taking a long sip.

Luna rubbed against my leg, then hopped back onto the armrest like I hadn't just disappeared all night. Completely unbothered. Typical.

I watched her settle in, stretching out with a yawn before flicking her tail over the edge.

I took a sip of water, the glass still cold in my hand, and let myself sink into the couch again. My body was tired, but my thoughts were still moving slow, lazy circles around the night I just had.

Cassian.

Everything about him was intense—his voice, the way he looked at me, the way he moved like he was always five steps ahead. And now, after one tequila-soaked night and one very distracting goodbye kiss, I was sitting here wearing clothes he had ordered to be delivered to the penthouse, special for me, like it was the most normal thing in the world.

It all felt so easy.

Too easy.

Knowing Sienna wouldn't be arriving for at least an hour, I ended up doing what I always did when there was too much on my mind: I cleaned.

Not deep-cleaning. Just a light reset. Blanket over the back of the couch. Dishes in the sink. The kind of small domestic wins that made me feel like I had my life together.

Luna trailed behind me for a bit before getting bored and making her way to the windowsill, where she could judge the world in peace. I was halfway through making the bed when my phone buzzed again.

I wiped my hands on my leggings and grabbed it off the nightstand.

Unknown Number
[1 Attachment]

I frowned.

No message. Just a photo.

I tapped it open, expecting a meme or maybe spam.

But it wasn't that.

It was me.

Taken from outside the window.

From the sidewalk.

In the exact clothes I was wearing **in that moment.**

I blinked, heart stopping for a second. My mouth went dry.

The angle was wide, like whoever took it had zoomed in from the street. The image wasn't crystal clear, but it didn't need to be.

I stepped slowly toward the window, trying to keep my breathing steady.

There was no one outside. Just a parked car and the rustle of wind through a neighbor's wind chimes.

I backed away from the glass, pulling my curtains shut in a silent panic. My phone stayed clutched in my hand, thumb frozen over the screen.

The dots blinked across the bottom of the message thread like the sender was typing, my heart pounding with anticipation.

Then they vanished.

No follow-up. No message. Just that one picture.

I locked the phone and set it face down on the counter, refusing to look at it again.

It was probably a prank. Some sick, random glitch. Some asshole with the wrong number. Right?

Right.

Luna meowed softly and nudged her head against my leg, like she could feel the shift in me.

I forced a breath and reached down to scratch behind her ears, my fingers slightly colder than before.

Sienna would be here soon.

It was probably nothing.

Probably.

The knock at the door made me jump.

I blinked down at the phone still facedown on the counter, heart thudding a little too hard in my chest. For a second, I just stood there, unmoving. Then I heard it again—two quick knocks, followed by a familiar voice through the door.

"Don't make me stand out here holding iced coffee like some desperate caffeine delivery girl!"

Sienna.

I exhaled a laugh and practically sagged in relief.

"Coming!" I called, brushing my fingers through my hair as I crossed the room and unlocked the door.

Sienna breezed in the moment it cracked open, oversized sunglasses perched on her head, two drinks in hand, and an expression that said, you better give me something good.

"I brought fuel," she announced, handing me one of the cups. "And a blueberry muffin I fully intend to share, but only if you're honest about last night."

I took the drink with a grateful nod. "You are an angel among mortals."

"I know," she said breezily, flinging her shoes off as she made herself at home. "And don't try to distract me with flattery."

Sienna flopped onto the couch, kicked her feet up like she lived here. "Okay," she said, sipping on her own. "I was going to start with something casual, but screw that—are you seriously not going to tell me where the hell you were all night?"

I blinked. "I texted you."

"*After* you reappeared from the void like nothing happened," she shot back. "You ghosted me for twelve hours, Kennedy. I was two seconds from filing a missing person's report and slapping your face on a milk carton."

I winced. "I didn't mean to disappear. Things just… escalated."

Sienna's eyes narrowed. "Escalated?"

I took a long sip of coffee.

She leaned forward, resting her elbows on her knees. "So… you spent the night with him. Did you guys hook up?"

Smirking, I shook my head. "What kind of girl do you think I am?"

"Well, considering you spent the night, which is already not like you, I thought you were gettin' some! My bad!" She put her hands up in the air in offense, then laughed.

I huffed. "That's fair."

She pointed her straw at me. "So? Spill. Was it actually good, or am I going to have to stab him later?"

I took another sip of my coffee, then gave her a quick rundown—how we ended up at his place, the tequila, the dancing, the kiss... and, yes, the part where I very gracefully threw up in his bathroom like a college freshman.

By the time I finished, Sienna had her hand over her mouth, trying not to spit out her drink.

"You did *not*."

"Oh, I did. Full-on tequila betrayal. It was humiliating."

She lost it, laughing so hard she actually doubled over. "God, I love you. You finally have a hot night with a hot guy, and your stomach is like, 'Nope. Time to ruin everything.'"

I groaned. "Don't remind me."

"No, seriously. That's peak you. You couldn't just let it be sexy—you had to humble yourself halfway through."

I flipped her off with no heat, and she grinned.

"Honestly?" she said, biting back a smile. "That sounds like a solid compatibility test. If he didn't bail after that, maybe he's worth a second date."

"And then," I added, "he kissed me the next morning. Outside my car. Fully sober, fully dressed, no tequila involved."

She sat back, sipping her coffee like she was trying not to look too impressed. "That's... actually kind of hot. Like, responsible hot."

I laughed. "That's a thing now?"

"Oh, absolutely. We're grown. Hot is emotional intelligence and clean dishes."

I laughed softly, leaning back against the couch, letting the caffeine and comfort settle into my limbs. Luna jumped up beside me, curled into a ball like she hadn't judged me all morning.

For a moment, everything felt... good.

Normal.

Sienna reached into the bag and pulled out a muffin, casually tearing off a chunk. "Oh—before I forget. This girl came into the shop this morning while I was working. Ordered through the app, but the name threw me."

I turned toward her. "Why?"

She handed me the crumpled receipt.

"Elara Royal."

The lightness drained from my chest.

I didn't say anything.

Just stood up and walked down the hall.

I knew where it was—had always known, even if I hadn't touched it in years. The box was wedged in the far back corner of my closet, tucked behind old sweaters and a shoebox full of tangled chargers. Out of sight. Where I meant it to be.

I reached up and pulled it down carefully, like it might break in my hands. It was small and plain—worn cardboard, the edges soft and slightly crushed. I had taped it shut once, like I could seal the memories inside. But I'd peeled that tape off a long time ago. I couldn't help myself.

There wasn't much in it. A few photos of my mom and me. A faded hospital bracelet I could never bring myself to throw out. And the letter.

The letter was always on top.

I just never had a reason to show anyone. Until now.

When I came back into the living room, Sienna had set her drink down. She didn't say anything, but her eyes tracked the box in my hands like she already knew it meant something.

I sat across from her and set it on the coffee table.

She looked at it, then at me. "What is that?"

"My mom's," I said. My voice came out softer than I expected. "Sort of."

Sienna didn't press. Just waited.

I opened the box and moved aside the things that didn't matter right now. My fingers brushed the edges of the letter, creased, familiar, already half-opened like it had been waiting for this moment too.

I hesitated. Not because I didn't trust Sienna. But because once she read it, she'd know everything.

And maybe I wasn't ready for *everything* to be known.

But I was tired of carrying it alone.

I unfolded the letter slowly and cleared my throat, eyes scanning down until I found the part that had etched itself into my memory years ago.

My voice was quiet when I read it out loud.

—her name is Elara. I don't know what she looks like. I don't know if she likes books the way you do, or if she has your temper, or your laugh—but she's your sister. Her mother's name is Dana. I found the birth certificate hidden in your father's briefcase when you were twelve. He never told me about her. Not really. Not until it was too late to change anything.

I wanted to leave, Kennedy. God, I wanted to. But I was already sick, and you were just a child. And I didn't want you to lose everything. I thought maybe… maybe if I stayed, you'd still have a father. Even if he was already giving pieces of himself to someone else.

Your sister, she doesn't know about us. I doubt she even knows I exist. But if you ever meet her, be kind. None of this is her fault.

The words felt heavier out loud than they ever did in my head.

When I finished, I didn't look up right away. I just folded the letter back along its creases and set it in my lap like that might somehow soften the ache in my chest.

The silence that followed stretched long and thick.

Then, finally—"What the actual fuck."

I looked up.

Sienna was staring at me, wide-eyed, coffee forgotten in her hand. "Kennedy."

Sienna stared at me, blinking like she wasn't sure she'd heard me right.

Then, quietly—"He had a whole other family... while your mom was dying?"

I nodded.

Her mouth opened, then closed. When she finally found the words, they were rough around the edges.

"What the fuck, Kennedy. That's not just awful, that's—" She cut herself off, running a hand through her hair. "I don't even have a word for how fucked that is."

She looked at me again, like she was trying to keep herself from coming completely unglued.

"I'm sorry. I just... I don't get how someone does that. To your mom. To you."

Sienna stared at me, stunned into silence. Her eyes flicked to the letter in my lap, then back up to my face.

She swallowed. "Kennedy..."

I shook my head before she could say anything else. "It's fine."

"It's not."

Her voice was soft now. No anger, no edge—just quiet disbelief. Like she was still trying to wrap her head around it.

I could see the war on her face—part of her wanted to say something, to scream about how screwed up it all was. But instead, she just leaned forward, rested her elbows on her knees, and looked at me like I was the only thing in the room.

"How long have you known?"

"A while," I said. "Before she died. She left the letter hidden in one of her books."

"And you've just... kept it?"

I nodded.

Sienna didn't say anything right away.

Then—softer—"You have a sister."

I nodded, staring down at the letter in my hands.

And for the first time since reading it, the truth of it settled somewhere in my chest.

HAILEY M. BERTOLDI

I have a sister.

Kennedy

8

W e didn't talk about the letter again—not because it didn't matter, but because some things are too big to touch right away. It wasn't avoidance. It was space. A quiet understanding between two people who knew that sometimes, silence could hold more than questions ever could.

So we did what we do when life knocks the wind out of us. We opened a bottle of wine and tried to remember how to breathe. I pulled two mismatched glasses from the cabinet and filled them halfway—any more and I knew Sienna would side-eye me like I didn't know my own limits. She had already thrown on the oversized hoodie she kept at my place and kicked off her shoes like she owned the apartment. Luna had curled up at her side, blissfully unaware of family secrets and emotional detonations. I climbed onto the couch beside her, tucked my legs beneath me, and held out her glass.

"To family secrets and overpriced wine," I said, raising my glass. Sienna clinked hers against mine. "And the best friend who makes both survivable."

We drank.

The movie we put on was ridiculous. Something about a fake wedding, a secret prince, and at least three slow-motion eye contact scenes. We didn't care. It filled the space.

Between scenes, we talked.

Not about Elara. Not about Michael. But about everything else.

Sienna launched into a rant about the espresso machine acting possessed again. I told her about the time I almost sliced my finger off trying to pit an avocado. She reminded me that I once dated a guy who thought cryptocurrency was a personality trait.

I laughed so hard I snorted wine through my nose.

By the time we were deep into our second glasses, my shoulders had loosened and so had the knot in my chest. Not completely—but enough.

"You ever think about what she's like?" Sienna asked at one point, voice soft.

I knew she meant Elara. I stared at the wine in my glass, watching it shift as I swirled it once, slowly. "Sometimes."

Sienna didn't press. She just nodded, her knee brushing mine. "If she's anything like you, she's probably already running the world."

"Or setting it on fire."

"Same thing."

We both smiled.

The warmth of the room wrapped around us like a blanket—wine, candlelight, the soft flicker of a feel-good movie no one was really watching. It felt like something close to peace. Or as close as I'd been in a while.

Eventually, we fell into that soft kind of quiet that only exists between people who don't need to fill the air with anything. Luna shifted in her sleep, tail twitching once.

I exhaled, leaned back, letting my eyes drift shut for a second.

Then my phone buzzed from across the room. Neither of us moved at first.

Sienna reached for it with lazy fingers. "Want me to check—"

She froze. Her whole body went still.

I opened my eyes and looked over at her. She was staring at the screen. The color drained from her face.

"…Kennedy?"

Kennedy

9

I stared at the photo, taking my phone from her hand as my pulse hammered in my ears. It was unmistakable: my front door, a wilted rose lying carelessly on the welcome mat. The image was too specific, too intimate. It was a message—letting me know I'm being watched, closely. The chill that ran through me wasn't just from the cold air in the room. It was real, sinking deep into my bones.

Sienna's gaze drifted, a million miles away. The silence stretched, thick and suffocating, waiting for someone to make sense of it. She leaned in towards me, squinting at the photo, her brow furrowed as if she could somehow will it to be something else—something that didn't feel so wrong. But there was no denying it.

"What the fuck is that, Ken?" Sienna's voice cracked through the silence, sharp and low. Then her eyes flicked up to mine, searching for answers. But I didn't have any. I couldn't say anything. The words wouldn't come.

My hands shook as I placed the phone down carefully, as if it might explode if I didn't. Slowly, I searched for the postcard—the one I'd left on my entryway table, hoping it would just disappear, hoping I could ignore it. Finding it under a small stack of mail, the edges frayed and familiar, I brought it to Sienna without a word.

She grabbed it, scanning the handwriting, her eyes moving between the postcard and me. She blinked a few times, as though trying to process what she was seeing. She didn't have to ask—she knew. I knew. We both knew.

"It's happening again," I said, my voice quiet but calm, too calm. I couldn't bring myself to feel anything more than a quiet, gnawing dread.

Sienna was silent, her expression distant as she tried to make sense of things. She just stared blankly at me, the weight of the moment sinking in. Then her face twisted, disbelief spreading across it like a cloud.

"Are you sure? I mean, are you sure it's the same person?"

I shrugged, my throat tightening. But it didn't make sense to question it. I didn't need to say the words. It was the same feeling. The same fear that had gnawed at me when I was in college. The same paranoia that crept in when I least expected it.

Sienna's eyes went wide, her voice hoarse. "It's been years... why now?"

I didn't answer. I had no clue. The knot in my stomach was too tight, and I wasn't sure I could even breathe properly.

But Sienna wasn't done. She took a step closer, her voice urgent now. "Kennedy, we have to tell your dad. You know that, right?"

I swallowed hard, feeling the weight of her words settle around me. She was right.

"I don't want to tell him," I said quietly, my voice tight with uncertainty. "He doesn't even care about me—why would he care about this?"

Sienna's eyes softened, but her tone remained firm. "You're wrong. Michael might not be the dad you want him to be, but he's got power. He has connections. He can do something."

I shook my head, frustration bubbling up. "You think he'll care? He's been so wrapped up in his own world, in his other family, that I barely exist to him. How can I expect him to actually help now?"

Sienna didn't back down. "Because this isn't just about you anymore. It's about your safety. And the cops?" She shook her head, eyes full of understanding. "They won't do shit, you know that! But Michael? He can make things happen. He's got the influence. If you tell him, at least you have someone who can actually protect you."

I hesitated, the knot in my stomach tightening further. "But what if he doesn't do anything? What if he just brushes me off?"

Sienna stepped closer, her voice soft but unwavering. "At least you'll know you tried. And if he does care, even a little, he can handle it. He has the resources."

I exhaled sharply, feeling the weight of her words. She was right about one thing—the cops wouldn't do anything without proof. But Michael could. And that terrified me—because I knew what he was capable of... Before I could speak, my phone buzzed on the table. The familiar ping echoed in the silence, and I already knew who it was.

Cassian.

Sienna's gaze flickered to the screen, then back at me. "You gonna answer that?"

I glanced down, and there it was:

Cassian: *Miss your face! Did Sienna burn down the shop?*

A small smile tugged at the corner of my mouth. Typical Cassian. Even with everything swirling around me, he managed to break through the chaos, grounding me for just a moment.

Sienna, watching me carefully, didn't need to ask. "What's that about?"

I barely glanced up, keeping my tone casual. "Nothing. Doesn't matter."

"Is it Cassian?" Her voice was quieter this time, but there was an edge to it—like she already knew the answer.

My head snapped up, and I met her gaze, my stomach twisting. "Why does it matter?"

Sienna's brows shot up. "Why does it matter?" She took a step closer, her arms crossing tightly over her chest. "Ken, don't you think the timing is a bit convenient? Right after that picture was sent, he decided to check in? He could have done that hours ago!"

I blinked, my throat tightening. "You're reading too much into it," I said, forcing the words out, but they came sharper than I meant.

Sienna's eyes narrowed, her concern deepening. "Am I? No, I don't think you're paying enough attention."

I looked away, focusing on the phone in my hand, my pulse pounding in my ears. "Please stop." My voice was low, a quiet warning.

But she didn't.

"No, Kennedy." Her voice was harder now, her frustration bleeding through. "If you aren't going to take this shit seriously, I will. Maybe Jaxon was right—maybe there's something off about him."

My head jerked up, and this time, the heat in my chest burned through the exhaustion.

"Stop."

The word came out cold. Sharper. A warning no longer—this was a line. Sienna's eyes widened, but I wasn't finished.

"Why do you always pull this shit?" My voice was steel, slicing through the tension. "Every time I try to have a life outside of you and Jaxon, you act like I'm abandoning you. Like I'm not allowed to be happy unless it's on your terms."

Sienna blinked, her mouth opening slightly, but I kept going.

"You don't want me to move on." My voice cracked, but I forced it out anyway. "You and Jaxon—neither of you do. You just want me stuck here, waiting around for when you need me."

"Ken, that's not—"

"Don't." My voice was ice now, the weight of it pressing down on both of us. "Just... stop."

The silence that followed was suffocating.

Sienna's jaw clenched, her eyes full of hurt and frustration. But I didn't care. Not anymore.

"I need space," I muttered, barely able to meet her eyes. "Please."

Sienna's lips parted, and for a second, I thought she was going to walk away. But then she spoke, and her voice was sharp, cutting through the air like a blade.

"Space?" She scoffed, her eyes narrowing. "Are you kidding me right now?"

My jaw tightened. "Sienna—"

"No." Her tone was sharper now, laced with something close to disbelief. "Don't turn this around on me, Ken. You're shutting me out because it's easier than admitting something's off."

I looked away, focusing on the phone in my hand, my pulse pounding in my ears.

"Every time someone tries to look out for you, you push them away." Her voice was low, but there was no softness left in it. "And for what? So you can lose yourself in someone who barely knows you?"

That hit a nerve.

My grip tightened around the phone. "You don't know him."

"Neither do you." Her eyes locked onto mine, her words cutting deeper. "But that doesn't seem to matter, does it?"

I swallowed hard, my throat tightening. "I'm not doing this with you."

"Yeah, you are." Sienna's voice was steady now—too steady. "Because I'm not just going to stand here and watch you pretend everything's fine when it's not."

My head snapped up, frustration boiling over.

"God, Sienna." The words exploded out of me before I could stop them. "Why can't you just let me figure this out for myself? You act like I'm some fragile little girl who can't make her own damn choices."

Sienna's jaw clenched, her eyes narrowing. "That's not what this is about, and you know it."

"Then what is it?" My voice was sharper now, cutting through the space between us. "Because from where I'm standing, it sure as hell feels like it!"

Her expression hardened, her arms crossing over her chest. "No. This is about you running headfirst into something dangerous because you don't want to be alone."

My pulse spiked, heat rising in my chest too fast to control.

"Shut up." My voice was low and unforgiving.

"That's what this is, isn't it?" Sienna's voice dropped, but the weight in her words was heavier. "You'd rather throw yourself at the first guy who gives a damn than deal with… everything."

My stomach twisted, and something sharp sliced through me.

"Fuck you." The words came out quieter than I expected, but they landed with a thud between us.

Sienna blinked, but I could see the hurt flash in her eyes before she masked it with anger.

"You're unbelievable," she murmured, her voice barely above a whisper.

I felt the heat rising again, the anger bubbling up too fast for me to contain it.

"Why don't you worry about getting your own life together, Sienna?" My voice was quieter now, but the bite was still there. "You hang out at the café because it's easier than admitting you don't know who the fuck you are without me."

Her jaw clenched tighter, but this time, she didn't speak.

And I should've stopped. I should've shut my mouth and let it go.

But I didn't.

"Or maybe," I said, voice cool and cutting, "you stick around to sneak around with Jaxon behind my back."

Silence.

Sienna didn't flinch.

Her lips curled slightly, but there was no humor behind it.

"Oh, you're finally ready to talk about that?" Her voice was cool, detached—like this wasn't about to destroy everything. "Because I was wondering how long it would take for you to figure it out."

She didn't wait for me to respond.

"Yeah, Ken. I fucked him." Her tone was flat. "And not just once."

"It started after you ditched him that night at the club. Remember that? When you ran off because everything was just too much and left him standing there like a fucking idiot?"

"He showed up at my place after." Her jaw tightened. "Pissed. Drunk. And I let him in. I shouldn't have. I know that. But I did."

"And you know what, Ken?" Her head tilted slightly, her eyes narrowing. "It was easy. Too fucking easy."

"Because he was tired of waiting for you to figure your shit out. Tired of being the backup plan. Tired of being treated like a fucking afterthought while you sat there feeling sorry for yourself."

"So yeah, Ken." Her lips pressed together for a beat before her tone dropped lower. "I fucked him."

"In my bed. On my couch. Against my fucking kitchen counter."

"And you know what?" Her brows lifted, her tone almost conversational now. "He didn't even hesitate."

"He was pissed. And I was there. And he…" She paused, but not for effect. "He needed to feel something that wasn't tied to you."

"And I gave him that."

"He told me things, Ken." Her eyes flashed, her jaw clenched. "About how he felt like a fucking idiot waiting for you to figure out if you even wanted him. About how he was sick of being strung along while you acted like you were too good to admit you wanted him."

"And you know what else?" Her lips curled, but there was no warmth in it. "He didn't feel like an idiot that night."

"Because I gave him what he *needed.* What you *never could.*"

"And yeah..." Her voice dipped lower, almost thoughtful now. "He liked it. A lot."

"Liked how I took him. Liked how I let him fuck me however he wanted."

"Liked how I didn't make him beg for it."

I was done listening.

"Get out."

My voice was low, but the force behind it was undeniable.

Sienna's head shot up, her eyes narrowing. "What?"

"Get. Out."

Her smirk faded.

For a moment, she just... stared, like she realized the severity of the argument.

"Ken—"

"Are you deaf?" I couldn't contain myself any longer, my jaw clenched so tight it hurt. "GET THE FUCK OUT!"

That did it.

She gathered her things in silence, her movements stiff and mechanical. As she reached the door, she hesitated—just for a second. I caught the glint of a tear in her eye, but I looked away before it could mean anything. The door slammed behind her, the sound echoing through the room and making my heart jump.

I let out a shaky breath, the silence pressing down like a weight.

My phone was still on the counter, so I reached for it. Cassian's message was waiting.

Cassian: *"Miss your face! Did Sienna burn down the shop?"*

My throat tightened as I stared at the message, my mind racing too fast to think.

Kennedy

10

T he sound of the door closing still echoed in my head, even though Sienna had been gone for minutes. The silence she left behind was unbearable, thick with everything that had been said.

My hands trembled as I looked down at my phone.

Cassian's message was still there. *"Miss your face! Did Sienna burn down the shop?"*

It wasn't the words that made me press his name. It was the fact that he was the only person who hadn't torn me apart tonight. The only one who didn't look at me like I was the problem.

My fingers hovered for just a second before I typed:

Me: *"Please tell me you're free right now."*

His response came almost instantly.

Cassian: *"Where are you? Getting in my car now."*

My fingers shook as I tapped out a quick reply.

Me: *Corner of Maple and Fifth."*

I didn't have to wait long. The minutes dragged as I stepped outside, the cool air biting my skin. My arms folded tightly across my chest as I stood on the curb, trying to hold everything together. The silence pressed in on me from all sides.

It was strange standing there, waiting for him, while the world kept moving. Cars passed by, oblivious to the turmoil swirling inside me.

But I didn't move. I just waited.

And then I saw him.

Cassian's sleek black car slowed as it pulled up to the curb. He was out of the car before I could take another breath, his eyes locking onto mine the second he saw me.

"Hey." His voice was softer than I expected.

I couldn't find the words, but I didn't need to.

I stepped closer, feeling Cassian's arms instantly wrap around me, warm, steady, and grounding me in a way I hadn't realized I needed. He didn't say anything. He didn't pry. He just held me, and I let myself sink into his chest.

The moment I slid into the passenger seat, everything felt lighter. It wasn't perfect—nothing could fix how I felt—but for the first time tonight, I felt like I could breathe. I wasn't sure what I expected, but it wasn't this.

We didn't talk about the fight with Sienna. We didn't talk about the postcards, the picture, or the feeling that someone was lurking just beyond my reach, watching me like I was some kind of prey. No, we didn't talk about any of that.

Instead, Cassian kept his eyes on the road, the music playing softly, every once in a while shooting me that smirk of his that somehow made everything feel easier.

"Are you ready?" he asked, glancing over at me with that familiar grin.

"For what?" I asked, raising an eyebrow, still unsure what he had in mind.

"To get your ass whooped," he said, trying to contain his laughter. "I'm taking you bowling."

I snorted. "Bowling?" I couldn't help but smile. "Are we twelve?"

He just shrugged, his grin wide. "Talk shit if you want to but I have a feeling you're a gutter ball queen."

We got to the bowling alley, and Cassian led the way with that same cocky swagger, even as he grabbed shoes and handed me a pair of bright red ones. Bowling was never my thing, but it was a distraction nonetheless. Something I could focus on other than the mess in my head.

"So, what's the strategy?" he asked, looking over at me while I laced up my shoes.

I glanced up at him, my lips twitching. "The strategy is winning. I don't plan on embarrassing myself."

He laughed. "Again, anyway."

My mouth fell open, knowing exactly what he was referring to. "You were just waiting to throw that in my face, huh?" I grinned, giving him a playful shove.

The banter was effortless, for a while, I forgot about everything. I could almost pretend things were normal. We laughed and joked about who could get the highest score, and when I missed a spare by a mile, Cassian was quick to make it known.

"Well, looks like an 'I told you so' is in order," he said with a grin after I threw the ball straight into the gutter.

"Not yet," I shot back. "The game's not over!"

We kept playing, the sound of the pins crashing almost like music to my ears. Cassian didn't push me to talk about anything. He just let me exist, teasing and joking, keeping my mind off everything weighing me down. It was exactly what I needed.

The time passed, and I was starting to feel more like myself, like the mess in my head didn't matter much. When I finally got a strike (after probably 10 failed attempts), I couldn't help but throw my arms up and grin at Cassian.

"Victory!" I shouted, laughing.

Cassian just raised his hands in mock defeat. "Damn it!"

I stuck my tongue out at him, basking in the glory. For once, I felt like I was living in the moment, not worrying about anything else. But as the game went on, I started to quiet down a bit, just taking it all in—the sound of the ball hitting the lane, the gentle hum of people laughing in the background. I didn't want to think too hard.

When it was over, and we were walking back to the car, I felt the weight creeping back in. It wasn't just a physical feeling—it was like the world had gotten too big for me, and I just wanted to sit in the quiet.

As we reached the car, Cassian looked over at me, his face serious but still gentle. "So, do you want to head home or do you want a change of scenery for the night?" He didn't make it sound like a big deal—just a casual offer, letting me choose. "No pressure either way."

I glanced over at him, considering. I wasn't ready to go back to an empty apartment. Maybe I could keep the distraction going a little longer.

"A change of scenery sounds nice," I said, my voice softer than I intended.

He nodded, not saying anything else, and we slid into the car. The engine started, and the low hum of the music filled the space between us. I wasn't sure if it was music or the quiet that helped, but it was a relief in its own way not to have to speak.

The drive was smooth, Cassian focused on the road, his eyes glancing over at me every once in a while, but he didn't push me to talk. It was as if he knew something had shifted, but he wouldn't force anything. For the first time in a while, I wasn't being bombarded with questions, I wasn't expected to explain myself. I just existed in the quiet.

But I could feel the heaviness in my chest, the echo of everything that had happened tonight. The weight of the fight with Sienna, the postcards, the picture—it was all still there, pressing down on me.

When we pulled into his parking garage, I didn't move right away. The car rolled to a stop, and the quiet stretched between us. Cassian killed the engine but didn't look at me. He let the silence sit there, as if he was giving me time to figure out what to do next.

I didn't know what to do. I felt the desire to be alone, but at the same time, I didn't want to be. I just wanted a few minutes to breathe, and it felt like I could do that here, with him.

When we arrived at his penthouse, Cassian led the way inside. The door clicked shut behind us, and for a moment, the weight of the night settled over me again. He moved toward the kitchen without saying anything, but I could feel his eyes on me. He wasn't pushing me to talk, but there was something there—a quiet understanding.

"Want a drink?" he asked, grabbing a bottle of whiskey.

I nodded, too tired to make any more decisions. Cassian poured two glasses, his movements casual but steady. I took mine from him, the cool glass feeling almost grounding against my fingers. I sipped the drink slowly, the warmth from the alcohol spreading through me, but it didn't erase the tightness in my chest.

Cassian didn't say anything at first. He just watched me, his eyes careful, like he was waiting for something to happen. The air between us was thick, almost heavy, but there was no pressure. He let me sit in the silence.

I took another sip, but the drink was just a distraction, and I was starting to feel more of the weight I'd been avoiding. The world felt like it was pressing in again, and I didn't want to be alone with those thoughts anymore.

I set my glass down, and without really thinking, I moved closer to him. He didn't stop me. He just watched, his eyes soft, waiting for me to make the next move.

And when I was close enough, I whispered, "I just want to be here. With you." I didn't know why those words came out—didn't know why I needed to say them. But they felt like the truth. I wasn't ready to face everything, to talk about what was suffocating me. I just wanted to be in this moment.

Cassian didn't ask anything more. He didn't press. He simply reached out, pulling me closer, and I sank into his warmth. For once, I didn't feel like I had to fight it. I let myself lean into him, feeling the tension slowly start to fade. Being here, in his arms, felt like pressing pause on everything unraveling around me. I didn't want to think. I didn't want to feel. I just wanted to forget.

I pressed my lips to his—soft at first, almost tentative, like I was testing the waters. But the second I started to pull away, Cassian's hand slid up, gently tangling in my hair as his lips found mine again, and this time there was nothing soft about it. His kiss was deep, consuming, and I gave in to it fully. I could feel the heat of him against me, his hands slipping under my dress, the touch of his skin against mine making me shiver. There was no hesitation between us now, no words needed.

He lifted me easily, moving us to the couch. I barely registered the motion, lost in the way his hands held me, in the way he kissed me like he needed me. When he pulled back, there was a moment of stillness—just the two of us, our eyes locked. I could feel the heat building between us, the tension thick in the air. Without breaking eye contact, he slowly helped me out of my dress, tossing it aside. My body was exposed to him, and I didn't feel vulnerable. I felt wanted, desired in a way that made me forget everything else. Cassian's eyes darkened, his breath quickening as he kissed me again, more urgently this time.

His hands moved over me, teasing, as he took his time undressing. I pulled him closer, my body aching for him, needing him. The moments passed in a haze of kisses, of touches, of desperate need. I felt his skin against mine, the intensity between us building with every second.

When he finally positioned himself over me, there was no more hesitation, no more questioning. His hands gripped my hips, guiding me closer to him. I wrapped my legs around him, pulling him in deeper, and he groaned against my lips as I did. The feeling of him inside me was more than just physical—it was everything I needed, everything I craved in that moment.

He moved with me, his rhythm steady, his focus entirely on me. Each thrust was slow, deliberate, and I responded in kind, our bodies moving together in perfect harmony. Every touch, every kiss was an affirmation that we were both lost in this, in each other.

As the moments stretched on, everything else faded away. There was no past, no fight, no fear. There was only him, only the connection between us that was raw and powerful. And when the wave finally hit, I felt like I was falling into something deep, something real, as Cassian's name escaped my lips in a breathless cry.

As the intensity faded, Cassian's body softened against mine, his breath still slow and steady. He didn't pull away immediately, just stayed close, resting his forehead on mine. The silence between us wasn't awkward; it was comforting, like everything had fallen into place.

I let my fingers trail over his back, tracing the outlines of his muscles. I didn't need to say much. My chest felt lighter, the weight of everything else easing.

Cassian's grin was impossible to miss as his hand trailed lazily along my side, his touch warm and grounding even as his breathing started to slow. "Well…" His voice was softer now, but that cocky glint was still there, making my stomach flutter. "Now I need food to recover. I think you just ruined me."

I snorted, burying my face against his shoulder as the laugh bubbled up. "You're impossible."

"And starving," he murmured, pressing a lingering kiss to my forehead. His lips curved into a smirk against my skin. "But I'd let you ruin me again if it means I get to do that all over." My heart flipped in my chest, the weight of the night feeling a little lighter. And for the first time in a while… I smiled.

Cassian's eyes softened as his hand brushed gently over my cheek, his thumb tracing lazy circles before he leaned down and pressed a soft, lingering kiss to my lips—one that tasted more like a promise than a goodbye. When he finally pulled back, his grin was back in full force. "Now I *really* need food," he murmured, his lips brushing mine one last time. "Unless you're offering something sweeter."

I rolled my eyes, but the smile tugging at my lips betrayed me. "Tempting..." My voice was softer than I intended, and the warmth still lingering between us made it hard to think straight.

But I didn't pull away. I couldn't.

Instead, I leaned in, brushing my lips against his one more time—just a soft, lingering kiss that tasted of everything I wasn't ready to say.

"But I think you'll have to settle for actual food," I murmured, my lips barely grazing his as I pulled back, feeling the flutter of his breath on my skin.

Cassian's grin widened as I pulled away, his eyes flickering with something darker—something I wasn't ready to confront. But he didn't push.

"Actual food it is, then." His voice was lighter, but there was no mistaking the quiet satisfaction lacing his tone. Like he knew exactly what he'd just done to me—and how much I liked it.

Cassian didn't rush as he stood, his movements slow and deliberate, like a man who had nothing to prove but still owned the room. He grabbed his boxers, sliding them on with an easy confidence that made it impossible not to watch. His body was all hard lines and effortless control, and the way his muscles flexed with each subtle movement sent a shiver down my spine.

His grin was back in full force as he glanced at me over his shoulder, his voice dripping with cocky satisfaction. "Careful, sweetheart…" His lips quirked as his eyes darkened. "Look at me like that for too long, and I might forget about the food."

I swallowed hard, my throat suddenly dry as heat flared low in my stomach.

He reached for his phone, his fingers moving lazily over the screen as he placed an order, but I could feel it—his awareness of me never wavered. Even with his back turned, Cassian was still in control, still commanding every inch of the space around him.

And damn it… I liked it.

I pulled the blanket from the back of the couch, wrapping it around my shoulders as the warmth settled over me. The air between us was softer now, comfortable in a way that made my chest ache. Cassian was still beside me, his body close but not overwhelming, his attention focused on his phone as he finished placing the order. It should have been easy to settle, but my thoughts were still tangled in everything that had happened tonight.

I tucked my knees up beneath the blanket, sinking deeper into the cushions. My body was finally starting to relax, but my mind wouldn't stop spinning. The weight of the fight with Sienna still lingered, tangled with everything I didn't want to think about right now.

The silence stretched between us, soft and easy. I wasn't in a hurry to fill it, and neither was Cassian. He let me exist in that quiet, giving me space without pushing for anything more.

When he finally set his phone down, I felt his eyes on me before I heard his voice.

"So…" Cassian's tone was low, smooth, but there was that familiar edge of amusement beneath it. His gaze flicked toward me, his lips curling into that signature smirk that always managed to make my stomach flip. "Why were you so hasty to see me tonight?"

My heart skipped, and I bit the inside of my cheek, trying to ignore the way his voice made warmth bloom beneath my skin.

I shifted beneath the blanket, my fingers brushing the edge of the fabric as I looked down, avoiding his gaze. "Sienna and I… we got into a pretty bad fight."

Cassian's brow lifted slightly, but he didn't press. He just waited—patient, steady, giving me space.

"About you," I murmured, my throat tightening as I forced the words out.

Cassian's smirk deepened, a glint of amusement flickering in his eyes. "Ah." His voice was softer now, but there was something dangerous in the way he said it—like he already knew how this story was going to end. "Let me guess…" His head tilted slightly, his eyes narrowing just enough to make my pulse skip.

"Jaxon thinks I'm bad for you, and Sienna's convinced I'm going to ruin your life?"

I tried not to smile, but the corner of my mouth betrayed me. "Something like that."

Cassian chuckled softly, his eyes darkening just enough to make my stomach flutter. "I'm starting to think your friends don't like me very much."

I could've left it there. I should've. But something about the quiet comfort of this moment made it too easy to let my guard slip.

"It wasn't just about that..." My voice was softer now, almost hesitant. "Sienna thinks I'm... rushing into things."

Cassian didn't react right away. His silence stretched between us, but it wasn't uncomfortable. It was intentional, like he was giving me room to say more if I wanted to. But there was something beneath that patience—something that felt like control.

"She thinks I'm not thinking things through," I murmured, my throat tightening as I remembered Sienna's words. "That I'm... getting too caught up."

Cassian's smirk faded slightly, but his expression remained calm—too calm. His thumb brushed lazily over the back of my hand, grounding me. "And what do you think?"

His voice was low, steady, but there was something beneath it... something almost dangerous in the way he asked.

I swallowed hard, my heart pounding a little too fast. "I think..." I exhaled slowly, forcing myself to meet his eyes. "I think Sienna doesn't understand."

Cassian's eyes darkened, but his smirk was back, softer this time. "Good," he murmured, his lips brushing against my forehead in a way that made my stomach flip. "Because I'm not going anywhere."

I tried to ignore the way my heart skipped at his words—the way that playful edge in his voice made it too easy to forget everything else.

But then Cassian's hand drifted down, his fingers tracing lazy circles against my skin, his touch warm and grounding.

"Maybe..." His voice was softer now, thoughtful in a way that made my pulse slow. "Maybe you're right."

I blinked, lifting my eyes to meet his. "About what?"

Cassian's smile was gentle, but there was something **calculated** beneath it—something I couldn't quite place.

"About Sienna not understanding." His thumb brushed over my knuckles, soothing but firm. "Maybe you and Sienna... and Jaxon... just need a little space. To cool off. Clear your heads."

My throat tightened, but Cassian's touch was still there, steady and comforting. "I don't know..." My voice was barely above a whisper, uncertainty curling around the edges of my thoughts.

"Just for a little while," Cassian murmured, his eyes never leaving mine. "Let things settle. Give yourself some breathing room."

I swallowed hard, the warmth of his words wrapping around me like a cocoon. It sounded… reasonable. Logical, even.

And after the way things ended with Sienna… maybe he was right, but the ache in my chest wouldn't go away.

"I just…" My voice was softer now, barely louder than a whisper. "What if I lose them?"

Cassian's hand stilled, just for a second. But then his thumb resumed its slow, steady circles over my skin, calm and grounding.

"You won't." His voice was softer this time, but there was a certainty in it that made my stomach flip.

My throat tightened, and I forced the words out before I could second-guess them. "What if they think I'm giving up on them?"

Cassian's lips brushed against my temple, and when he spoke, his words were softer, quieter.

"If they love you, they'll give you the time you need to sort yourself."

The ache in my chest didn't disappear, but it shifted—lighter now.

Cassian's hand never left mine, his thumb tracing slow, lazy circles that sent shivers down my spine. But instead of pushing for more, he leaned back slightly, his smirk returning—that dangerous glint back in his eyes.

"Okay," he murmured, his tone shifting, lighter now. "Enough serious talk for one night."

I blinked, surprised by the sudden change in his tone. "What?"

Cassian's grin was pure mischief as his fingers brushed over mine. "You need a distraction, Wildfire."

My breath caught. **That name.** It wasn't casual. It felt... different. Like he saw something in me I wasn't ready to face.

"And what exactly do you have in mind?" I asked, trying to keep my voice steady.

Cassian's smirk deepened, his eyes dancing with amusement. "I don't know... but I'm thinking of dessert. And I'm not talking about food."

My stomach flipped, but I laughed, the tension in my chest easing just enough to make me forget everything else.

"Jeez, you're ridiculous."

"Don't act like you don't want more." His grin was wicked, but his voice was softer now, pulling me back in. "Come on, Wildfire. Let me distract you."

And just like that... I forgot everything else.

Kennedy

11

For a moment, everything was quiet.

The tension from earlier was gone, replaced by the steady rhythm of Cassian's breathing beneath my cheek. His warmth wrapped around me, grounding me in a way that made the chaos of the night feel like a distant memory. I should have been thinking about everything that happened—every unanswered question and every shadow that still lingered—but I wasn't.

Instead, I let myself sink into him. My body felt heavy, but not in a bad way. It was the soft weight of surrender, of finally letting go. My head rested against his chest, the faint, steady beat of his heart lulling me more effectively than any promise of safety could.

Cassian's hand brushed lazily along my side, his touch softer now, almost absent-minded. He wasn't in a rush. He never was. And somehow, that made it easier to stay.

"You don't have to go home tonight, you know…"

The words were quiet, barely louder than the hum of the city beyond the glass, but they settled over me like a blanket—warm, steadying, safe.

My lips brushed against his skin when I murmured back, "I hadn't planned on it."

The admission slipped out before I could second-guess it. And maybe… I didn't want to.

Cassian pressed a kiss to the top of my head, his voice low enough to raise goosebumps along my arms. "I probably wouldn't have let you leave, anyway."

The rest of the night blurred together in fragments—warmth, his breathing steady against mine, the rare peace of not running from anything. For once, I didn't fight it. For once, I let myself stay.

Morning came too quickly.

Sunlight filtered through the blinds in pale gold stripes, cutting across the sheets and Cassian's bare skin. For a long time I stayed still, tangled in warmth that wasn't mine but felt like it could be. His arm draped across my waist, heavy and certain, like he had no intention of letting me go.

I should've moved. I should've slipped out of bed, gone home, gotten ready for work like a responsible adult. But when his breath brushed the back of my neck, slow and even, I closed my eyes again and let myself have just one more minute.

One minute turned into ten. Then twenty. By the time I finally sat up, I was half-laughing, half-cursing myself as I pulled on my shoes.

"I need clothes," I sighed, shaking my head as I laced my sneakers. "Last time you somehow had things waiting for me. This time I'd like to avoid round two of being rescued by your over-preparedness."

Cassian's lips curved into that calm, infuriating smirk. "You didn't seem to mind."

"I didn't have much of a choice," I shot back.

"Then let's get you clothes," he said simply, as if the matter were already settled.

I rolled my eyes, but there was a smile tugging at my lips. "Quick stop. Then coffee. I can't function without it."

Cassian hummed—low, knowing, like he was already ten steps ahead of me.

The city was already buzzing when we stepped outside, sunlight glinting off glass and metal, traffic carrying on like nothing had changed. For a while, I let myself believe it.

That illusion lasted all the way to my apartment door.

Luna's chirp echoed before I even unlocked it, sharp and scolding, like she'd been waiting all night just to give me a lecture.

"I know, I know," I murmured as soon as she wove between my legs, tail flicking in irritation. I scooped her up, pressing a kiss to the top of her head. "I'm the worst."

Cassian leaned against the doorway, jacket slung over his shoulder, expression unreadable. But when Luna melted into my arms, purring like she'd forgiven me already, I caught the smallest twitch at the corner of his mouth—like he was holding back a smile.

I set her down and gestured toward my bedroom. "Give me five minutes."

The sound of fabric zipping and hangers clattering filled the space as I stuffed clothes into a duffel bag—jeans, tops, a couple of dresses. Mundane motions in a life that felt anything but mundane. For a fleeting moment, I could almost pretend Cassian was just anyone waiting in my living room.

But Cassian was never just anyone.

When I came back out, my duffel bag slung over my shoulder, he was no longer by the door. He'd been claimed. Luna perched in his lap like she owned him, his long fingers moving absently along her back. The sight tugged something deep in my chest, and for the first time that morning, I smiled without hesitation.

"Ready?" I asked, adjusting the strap of my bag.

His eyes flicked to me, then down at Luna. "Ready."

He scooped her up effortlessly, tucking her against his chest like it was second nature. The sight alone made my brain short-circuit.

"What... are you doing?" I asked, half in disbelief.

He glanced up, smirk tugging at the corner of his mouth as Luna purred, shamelessly content.

"If she comes with us..." His gaze locked on mine, that dangerous glint hidden behind a deceptively soft tone. Calculated. Sweet. "You'll have no reason to leave."

Cassian shifted Luna against his chest and reached for the door but stopped mid-motion. His hand hovered just above the handle, still as stone. I frowned, following his gaze—and then I saw it.

A postcard. Thin cardstock shoved halfway beneath the door, the edge catching on the welcome mat. It hadn't been there when we came in. My stomach flipped so violently I swore the floor tilted under me.

Cassian crouched, his movements deliberate, controlled. He balanced the cat easily in one arm as he plucked the card from the floor with the other. For a moment he just stared at it, his jaw ticking once, sharp as a blade.

Luna gave a restless chirp, wriggling against his arm. He set her down without looking, and she trotted off with her tail flicking, blissfully unaware of the storm brewing above her.

Good morning, Sweet Girl.
Did you tell your new friend about us?

The handwriting clawed at my chest. Familiar. Too familiar.

"Is there something you need to tell me?" His voice was calm, but there was a weight in it that pressed against my ribs like a vice.

I opened my mouth, but nothing came. My throat had gone dry, my heart climbing higher into my chest with every second he studied the postcard.

"It's nothing you need to worry about, I promise." The words scraped out, too fast, too shaky.

His eyes flicked to me, sharp, unblinking. "Nothing? Kennedy, don't lie to me."

My shoulders sagged, the fight draining out of me before it had even started. "I'm not...I—nothing's really happened." I stumbled over my words, voice barely audible. I gestured weakly toward the entryway table.

Cassian's gaze followed, and when he spotted it, something changed. The shift was subtle, but it rattled me more than if he'd shouted. His expression hardened, unease settling behind those green eyes like a storm taking root.

He turned back slowly, holding both postcards like evidence. "Two cards. Same hand. This isn't nothing. Not anymore." His thumb brushed the edge of the cardstock, but his stare was all for me.

His voice dropped lower, quieter—but sharper. "Someone's been watching you for a while, Ken, but something tells me you already knew that."

Silence pressed in. My pulse hammered in my ears, and every excuse I thought of crumbled before I could say it.

Cassian tilted his head slightly, eyes narrowing, his voice smooth but unyielding. "Care to fill me in?"

His gaze sharpened. Waiting. Demanding.

My chest constricted, but I forced the words out. "Stay here."

I crossed the room before I could lose my nerve, crouching beside the bookshelf where a plain box sat wedged against the back. My hands trembled as I pulled it free. The cardboard was worn, edges soft from being shoved away and forgotten, but I knew every inch of it. I had kept it hidden for years—proof of something I prayed I'd never have to explain.

I set it on the table between us and lifted the lid. Postcards, dozens of them, slid against one another in a neat, damning stack. Every one of them, same handwriting. Every one of them signed the same way.

Cassian's jaw tightened as he sifted through them, his silence heavier than any words.

"They started in college," I whispered, unable to look away from the box. "Once I moved back home, they stopped, but within the last several weeks I've been getting these again. And then... there was an airdrop message. The rose."

My voice faltered, but I forced myself to move. I crossed into the kitchen, every step heavier than the last, and pulled the wilted flower from where I'd shoved it into a glass. The petals had browned, curling in on themselves, but it still carried that faint, sickly-sweet scent of decay.

I set it down beside the stack of postcards.

Cassian's eyes flicked from the dead rose to the words scrawled across the cardstock, his expression unreadable. But the muscle in his jaw ticked once, hard.

For a long, charged moment, he said nothing. Then he exhaled slowly through his nose, a sound that felt closer to a growl than a sigh. His movements sharpened—controlled, precise, but brimming with a fury that had nowhere to go.

Without a word, he scooped up Luna, grabbed my duffel from where I'd left it on the floor, and slung it over his shoulder. When he finally spoke, his voice was low, edged with steel.

"Get your keys. We're leaving. Now."

I hesitated, startled by the sudden command.

His gaze cut to mine, fierce and unyielding. "Ken, don't argue. You're not staying here another night."

Cassian's knuckles whitened against the strap of the duffel, the only crack in his otherwise perfect composure. He didn't raise his voice—he didn't need to. The fury was there, simmering beneath the surface, aimed squarely at whoever had been circling me all this time.

It wasn't the volume of his voice that terrified me. It was the precision. Like he'd already decided what would happen if anyone touched me again.

My eyes flicked once more to the table—the wilted rose, the postcards, evidence I'd hidden away for years. Now that they were out in the open, I hated how exposed they made me feel. Like every secret I'd buried had claws, and Cassian had just seen them all.

He shifted Luna more securely against his chest, his gaze cutting back to me, sharp and final. "Keys, Ken."

The command landed like iron, leaving no space for protest. My fingers fumbled in the dish by the door until the keys jingled in my grip, the sound sharp and brittle in the silence between us. The apartment felt smaller somehow, walls pressing in, as if it knew I wouldn't be coming back the same.

Cassian opened the door, waiting only long enough for me to step through. His grip on the duffel was steady, Luna tucked easily against his chest, but I could feel the storm radiating off him in waves.

When he shut the door behind us, the click of the lock echoed louder than it should have—final, unforgiving. It sounded less like protection and more like a verdict.

For the first time in years, I felt the full weight of the secret I'd carried—and I wasn't sure if setting it down in front of him was relief, or the beginning of something far worse.

Kennedy

12

The penthouse felt different with Luna in it. I watched her prowl through the open space, tail flicking like she owned it, her paws silent against the polished floors as she mapped out the edges of her new world. She paused at the massive floor-to-ceiling windows, nose twitching at the faint hum of the city beyond, then darted toward a shadow in the corner as if it might hold some secret. She was curious. Bold. Completely unbothered.

I envied her for that.

My hands kept busy while she explored. Scooping litter into the sleek new box that had been delivered earlier, tearing into a brand-new bag of food, the packaging still stiff and unfamiliar compared to the half-crumpled ones I had at home. Even the toys—bright against Cassian's dark, curated space—looked out of place, but I set them down anyway until the living room felt less like a museum and more like somewhere a cat could belong.

I wanted it to feel normal. To pretend this was just another morning, just another routine. But the truth was, nothing about it was normal. I was in Cassian's penthouse, unpacking pieces of my life I hadn't planned to bring here, trying to carve out familiarity in a place that wasn't mine. The postcards, the rose, the weight in Cassian's eyes when he'd told me to get my keys—none of it belonged here either, yet it followed me like a shadow I couldn't shake.

Luna finally chose her spot, curling up in a golden patch of sunlight spilling across the rug, and for a moment the sight grounded me. Simple. Safe.

Cats didn't care about stalkers or secrets or whatever storm I'd dragged into this apartment. They only cared about warmth and food and love. Maybe I should have let myself be that simple too.

But I couldn't.

The silence of the penthouse pressed in as I lowered onto the couch, its cushions swallowing me whole. Too still. Too sharp. Even the hum of the city beyond the glass felt distant, like the world had been muted up here.

Cassian stood by the windows, jacket discarded over a chair, his shoulders straight, his profile etched against the skyline in light and shadow. He hadn't spoken since we came in. He didn't need to. The air around him thrummed with calculation, a man whose mind never stopped moving.

I wrapped my arms around myself, staring at Luna's slow-rising breaths. I wanted this to feel like safety. I wanted this to feel like a fresh start. But all I could think was how fragile it was—this illusion of normal I kept trying to build.

Finally, his voice broke through, calm but carrying that unmistakable edge. "How long do you think you can keep living like this?"

I blinked, startled. "Like what?"

He turned his head, green eyes catching the light. "Pretending it's not happening." His tone was calm, almost casual, but the words landed heavy. "We walked out of your apartment and left a stack of postcards and a dead rose on your table. That's not nothing, Ken. You've let it follow you this far."

My throat tightened. "I'm not letting it follow me. I'm just—" I swallowed hard. "I'm trying to live my life."

"Your life," he repeated slowly. "Running a shop. Walking home alone. Acting like someone out there doesn't already know your name, your face, your schedule." His gaze sharpened. "That isn't life, Ken. That's gambling."

Heat flared in my chest, defensive, stubborn. "So what? I'm supposed to just stop living? Shut down everything I've built because some asshole wants to rattle me?"

His jaw flexed, but his voice stayed low, steady as a blade. "I'm saying if you don't take this seriously, they'll do more than rattle you."

My nails dug into my palms as I straightened. "I've lived with this before. I've handled it before. You don't get to walk in and decide now what my life is allowed to look like."

Cassian's eyes didn't so much as flicker. "Handled it?" he repeated softly, and somehow that was worse than if he'd laughed. His voice stayed calm, measured, but every word pressed tighter. "Boxes hidden under shelves. Roses you pretend are just flowers. Postcards you never answered. That isn't handling it, Ken—that's denial."

I swallowed hard, heat crawling up my neck. "But I'm still living."

"Hardly. You're a walking target." His words were quiet, deliberate, but they landed like blows. He stepped closer, green eyes locking onto mine with that unnerving steadiness. "People like this don't just watch forever. They escalate. They test your edges until they find the one that breaks you. And when it does, it's too late to take it seriously."

I hated the chill that crept into my bones at his certainty. Hated even more the truth humming underneath it. "So what then?" I demanded, sharper than I meant to. "I just shut everything down? Lock my doors, hide out here, live in your shadow while you decide what's safe for me? That's not life either, Cassian. That's a cage."

For the first time, his jaw clenched. He didn't move closer, but I felt it anyway—the storm brewing under his skin, held in check by sheer will. "I'm not trying to cage you." His voice dropped lower, harder. "I'm trying to keep you safe."

The silence that followed buzzed against my skin, thick and electric.

Finally, I forced out a breath and shook my head. "I can't live afraid of every shadow. I won't. The café is mine. My work, my people—it's who I am. If you want to help me, you'll have to find a way that doesn't make me a prisoner."

Cassian studied me for a long moment, unreadable, before something eased—just barely—in his shoulders. "Then we'll do it differently," he said, like it was decided. "But don't confuse compromise with safety. If you insist on working, I'll make sure you're not alone. One way or another."

My pulse jumped. "A bodyguard standing in the corner? That's going to terrify customers, Cassian."

His mouth curved into the faintest smirk, but it didn't reach his eyes. "Then he won't look like a bodyguard. He'll blend in. Work the counter. Smile at old ladies if that's what it takes."

I let out a shaky laugh, half nerves, half disbelief. "You make it sound so simple."

"Simple," he echoed, voice flat but certain. "It's the only way you walk out of this safely."

Eyes wide listening, I just laughed under my breath. Because no matter how much I wanted to argue, a part of me—the part still trembling from the memory of those postcards—knew he wasn't wrong.

Once he had disappeared into his office to take a call, the decision to leave was already made. I needed space to breathe. My keys felt heavy in my pocket, my duffel still slung on the couch where he'd dropped it earlier. I told myself I just needed air, just needed something normal. I didn't need his permission for that.

The elevator ride down felt longer than it should have, every floor sliding past in silence. My reflection in the steel doors looked like a stranger—pale, hair pulled into a loose knot, eyes still rimmed with shadows from too many sleepless nights. I pressed my lips together, straightened my shoulders. If Cassian wanted me locked away like glass on a shelf, then this was my rebellion, small as it was.

By the time my shoes hit the sidewalk, the city was already awake. Honking horns, chatter from passersby, the faint scent of roasted chestnuts from a vendor on the corner. Life was happening all around me, loud and ordinary, and for the first time all morning, I could finally breathe.

The café smelled like home the second I walked in—coffee, cinnamon, the faint trace of vanilla syrup clinging to the air. Familiar. Comforting. Mine.

Izzy was already behind the counter, her hair tied back with a bandana, sleeves rolled to her elbows as she frothed milk with practiced ease. She glanced up at the bell, then did a double take when she saw me.

"Boss lady," she said, arching a brow. "Didn't think I'd see you today. Everything okay?"

"Fine," I lied, forcing a smile as I slipped behind the counter. "Just… couldn't stay away."

She gave me a look but didn't press, instead sliding a cappuccino toward a waiting customer. I busied myself restocking syrups and straightening mugs, my fingers itching for the rhythm of routine. Every hiss of steam, every clink of ceramic, smoothed the jagged edges inside me.

Normal. That's what I needed.

The morning rush trickled in slowly, a few regulars chatting at their usual tables, a couple of students hunched over laptops. The hum of conversation rose and fell like background music, blending with the grind of beans and the hiss of the espresso machine. I almost convinced myself I was okay.

Until the bell over the door rang again.

I glanced up automatically, expecting another familiar face. Instead, a boy—maybe ten, maybe younger—stood there, clutching a folded bill in one hand. His sneakers squeaked faintly on the tile as he crossed to the counter, eyes fixed on the floor.

"Hot chocolate," he mumbled, sliding the crumpled cash forward.

"Coming right up." I smiled, softening my voice the way I always did with kids, and passed the order back to Izzy.

But the boy didn't move away. He hesitated, chewing his lip, before pulling something from his pocket. A postcard. He held it out to me, not meeting my eyes.

"A guy gave me ten bucks to give this to you."

The world tilted. My fingers went numb as I took it, the cardstock cool and light against my palm, heavier than stone in my chest.

The handwriting scrawled across the back made my stomach seize.

Oh Sweet Girl, there's no escaping me. I am inevitable.

The café moved on around me, but it was all wrong. Every sound came warped and distant—the hiss of steam, the scrape of mugs, Izzy's voice calling out an order like it was miles away. My breath hitched in shallow bursts, my fingers going cold even as my pulse thundered in my ears.

For one awful heartbeat, I thought about tearing it in half. Pretending it had never existed. But my fingers wouldn't move. Because I knew better.

This wasn't just a message. It was a promise.

My chest locked, air stuttering shallow. My fingers trembled so violently the cardstock bent, cracking down the middle like it might splinter with me. I couldn't move. Couldn't breathe. Frozen, waiting for a strike I couldn't see.

The bell above the door chimed.

I didn't flinch. Didn't even turn my head.

But then—Cassian's voice, sharp with alarm. "Ken?"

My body jerked at the sound, like his voice had reached further than I could. His shadow cut across the tiles, long and deliberate, and then he was there. His gaze dropped to the postcard crumpled in my fist, then rose to my face. Whatever he saw hollowed him out, his entire posture shifting into something feral, urgent.

"Ken," he said again, lower, tighter, the syllable vibrating with warning.

The air collapsed in my chest. My knees buckled.

And before the ground could meet me, his arms did.

The postcard slipped from my grip, skittering across the tile like a weapon discarded. My body caved against him, shaking so violently it rattled through both of us. My fingers clawed at his shirt, twisting the fabric as if I'd drown if I let go.

Gasps rippled through the café. A cup clattered, a chair scraped sharply against the floor. Izzy's voice cut off mid-sentence, strangled by shock. The hum of conversation evaporated until silence pressed heavy, broken only by the ragged, humiliating sob tearing its way out of my chest.

"I can't—" The words broke apart on my tongue, splintering. "Cassian, I can't keep doing this—"

His arms locked around me, unmovable, pulling me tight to his chest. He angled his body like a shield, broad and unyielding, cutting off every curious stare, every whispered breath around us. His jaw brushed my hair as he bent low, voice rough, guttural, vibrating against my skull.

"You're not doing this alone. I'm here."

The sobs kept coming, jagged and raw, years of fear ripping free in a tidal wave I couldn't control. My face buried against him, the front of his shirt soaking with salt and shame. The world I'd held together by sheer force of will was gone, shattered in front of everyone.

"He's never going to stop," I gasped, every word broken, terrified. "He's never going to stop—"

Cassian's hold only tightened, steady, absolute, his breath hot against my temple. His voice wasn't soft—it was steel sharpened to a vow.

"Then neither will I."

And then—he lifted his head, his green eyes cutting across the room like blades. The weight of him filled every corner of the café.

"We're closed." His voice was low, lethal, but it carried like a gunshot. "Now."

Chairs scraped back. Conversations died. No one argued. They moved—quiet, quick, almost tripping over themselves as they gathered their things. Izzy stood frozen behind the counter, wide-eyed, until his gaze snapped to her too.

"Izzy." His tone softened just enough to thaw the ice, but the command was still there. "Go home. You're off until I say otherwise. Paid. Don't come back until I tell you it's safe."

Her mouth opened, then closed. "Are you serious? I can't just—"

"You can," Cassian said flatly. "And you will."

Izzy glanced at me, guilt twisting across her face in protest. "Kennedy…"

I forced myself to meet her eyes, though my vision blurred with tears. "It's okay, Iz. Really." My voice cracked, but I managed a nod. "Go home. Please."

Something in my tone must've convinced her, because she finally grabbed her bag. At the door, she paused, twisting the strap between her fingers. "If you need anything—anything at all—you call me. Okay?"

I tried to smile, but it didn't reach. "I will."

The bell gave a faint jangle as Izzy opened the door and stepped out. She glanced back, then pulled it shut behind her. A sharp click followed as she turned the key from outside, locking us in.

The silence that followed was almost piercing.

The sound of the lock hit me harder than it should have, sharp and final, like the world outside had been cut away. My chest caved under it. A sob tore loose before I could stop it, jagged and raw, and suddenly I was shaking again—breath shallow, vision swimming, the weight of everything pressing down until I thought I might splinter apart.

Cassian's hold tightened instantly, his arm unyielding around me, grounding me against the spiral. He bent close, his words meant for me alone, rough and fraying at the edges of his control.

The silence that followed was unbearable. Only my broken breathing filled it, ragged against the steady wall of Cassian's chest. My tears had dampened his shirt, clinging to him like I couldn't let go—and maybe I couldn't.

Cassian's arm tightened around me. "Come on," he murmured, guiding me toward the back. His tone was softer now, stripped of that edge he'd used to scatter the crowd, but the steel was still there underneath.

I let him lead me into the break room, the tiny space suddenly feeling too small, too fragile to hold what had just happened. He eased me down onto the couch shoved against the wall, then crouched in front of me, bracing his arms on his knees. His eyes locked on mine, steady, relentless.

"Breathe, Ken." His voice was quiet, low, but it carried like an order. "Just breathe."

I dragged in a shaky inhale, then another, though the air still burned in my chest. Cassian stayed right there, close enough that his presence cut through the panic clawing at me. Close enough that I could feel the heat radiating from him like a barrier.

When I finally steadied enough to speak, my throat felt raw. "Everyone saw…" The humiliation hit sharp and hot, curling in my stomach. "I broke down in front of everyone."

His gaze didn't waver. "Let them see."

My brow furrowed. "Cassian—"

"Let them see what it costs to live with this," he said, voice harder now, though not unkind. "Let them see what happens when someone crosses the line. You think they saw weakness, Ken? They saw what happens when you're hunted. And they saw me make it clear it ends here"

I shook my head, pressing trembling hands to my face. "It's not that simple."

Cassian reached forward, gently prying my hands away. His grip lingered, firm but careful, grounding me. "It's never simple. But I promise you this—" His eyes bore into mine, green burning like fire under glass. "Whoever thinks they're inevitable has no idea what they've just started."

The weight of his words hung between us, heavy and unshakable. For a moment, I almost believed him—that he could will the danger away by sheer force, that the fire in his eyes was enough to burn down whatever shadow was chasing me.

Kennedy

13

By the time we made it back to the apartment, I felt hollowed out—like the panic had wrung me dry and left nothing behind but shaking bones and a heartbeat I couldn't slow.

I dropped onto the couch, the cushions swallowing me too easily, like they wanted me gone. My arms folded around myself, a weak attempt at armor, but I couldn't shake the tremor in my hands. My body didn't feel like mine anymore—just a bundle of nerves sparking too fast, too loud.

Cassian didn't join me. He stood near the windows, shoulders squared, arms crossed, his profile cut in sharp lines against the city beyond. Watching. Always watching. The silence between us wasn't empty—it pressed down thick and suffocating, like he was holding back the whole storm inside him just to keep it from spilling over onto me.

I pressed my forehead to my knees, but it didn't block out the replay in my head. The scrape of chairs against the floor. The way the café went dead quiet, every pair of eyes fixed on me. The hot flush of shame crawled up my throat as I folded in on myself like a child. I could still feel the postcard slipping from my fingers, skittering across the tile like some kind of weapon I hadn't known how to hold.

They all saw me break. They saw every jagged piece I've spent years holding together finally come apart. And no matter how tightly I curled in on myself now, I couldn't stuff those pieces back where they belonged.

The weight of Cassian's gaze pressed on me even without looking. Steady. Relentless. Like he could keep me pinned together with sheer force of will.

Finally, his voice broke the quiet. "You should drink something."

I shook my head without lifting it. "I'm fine." The lie scraped like glass in my throat, dry and raw.

"You're not." His tone wasn't sharp, but there was no space left in it for argument. He said it like a fact carved in stone.

My laugh came out brittle. "Don't do that."

"Do what?"

I lifted my head just enough to meet his eyes, green and unblinking in the half-light.

"Look at me like I'm broken. Like I'm about to fall apart again." My voice cracked, but I forced the words through anyway. "I don't need your pity."

Cassian's jaw tightened, but he didn't look away. If anything, his gaze steadied, unyielding. "I don't pity you, I care about you." he said quietly.

His words sank into me like lead. For a second, the silence between us thickened, heavy with everything I wanted to scream and everything he refused to say.

I dropped my face back into my arms, wishing I could vanish into the cushions, into the floor, into anywhere but here.

The elevator chimed, a sound so ordinary it didn't belong in the heavy quiet.

Cassian's head turned sharply toward the door. His entire body shifted in an instant, coiled and alert, like every muscle had been waiting for this moment.

Then the door opened.

Michael stepped inside without hesitation, two men shadowing his heels like sentinels. He moved with that same practiced authority he always carried—the kind that bent spaces around him, made people shrink whether they wanted to or not.

"Dad?" The word slipped out before I could stop it — soft, uncertain.

His gaze didn't come to me first. It locked onto Cassian, fury sharp and calculated.

My eyes darted to Cassian, searching for something — recognition, reassurance, anything but his jaw had already gone tight, his eyes locked on Michael.

The air shifted, sharp and heavy, as if the room itself knew what I hadn't realized yet.

"This is what you call keeping her in line?" His tone wasn't loud, but it carried the kind of precision that cut deeper than shouting ever could. "One task, Cassian. One. And what do I hear instead? My daughter's display is already the hot topic across the city—embarrassing. Do you realize what that does to a man of my status? You've turned her weakness into my liability. You're allowing her to single-handedly sabotage my campaign. I won't have it."

Cassian didn't flinch. His jaw worked once, slow and tight, before he answered, voice steady but edged like steel. "While you're worried about votes, your daughter is in danger. I'm trying to protect her."

Michael gave a short, humorless laugh, stripped of warmth. "Protect? That scene today—in front of a cafe full of patrons—did you see a woman being protected? No. Instead you allowed them to see weakness. And weakness doesn't just stain her, it stains me. The name *Royal* is supposed to mean power. Strength."

Cassian shifted his stance, arms loose at his sides now, his voice dropping into something harder. "She's worth more than your name will ever be. She's your daughter, you prick."

Michael's words cut like blades, each one sharper than the last, but he wasn't even looking at me. He stood there, tearing into Cassian like I wasn't sitting ten feet away. Like I was just some fragile mess he could scold from across the room without ever meeting my eyes.

It struck me then how perfectly composed he always looked, even in moments like this. His suit pressed sharp enough to slice, his tie knotted without a flaw, not a single strand of his dark hair out of place. To anyone else, he'd look like a man in control—a leader, a candidate, someone you could trust to shake your hand and run your city. But his eyes ruined it. Cold, assessing, like every second spent on me or Cassian was a calculation, another piece being shifted on his board.

I sat frozen on the couch, caught between their fire. My mind scrambled to keep up, but nothing made sense. Why was Cassian standing so still, jaw locked like he'd been expecting this? Why did Michael sound less like a father and more like a man lecturing an employee who'd failed him?

Confusion knotted in my chest, choking me as my gaze bounced between them. None of this fit. None of this was normal.

Michael's eyes narrowed, his mouth curving into something that wasn't quite a smile but wasn't far from it either. "And since when do you care what she is?" His words slid across the room like oil—slick, poisonous, meant to stick.

The silence that followed was unbearable. My stomach twisted, sharp ache blooming in my chest as I glanced between them.

"You two..." My voice cracked, thin and hoarse, but I forced it out anyway. "You know each other?" My hands curled into the couch cushions, desperate for something solid. "What's going on?" I was trying to make sense of all the back and forth.

Cassian's jaw flexed, his silence screaming louder than words ever could. He looked at me, then away, like there was something on the tip of his tongue he couldn't—or wouldn't—say.

"Ken—" Cassian's voice was low, strained, almost urgent. "It's not what you think."

My chest tightened. I wanted to believe him. God, I wanted to.

But Michael's laugh cut him off. Smooth. Calculated. "It's exactly what she thinks."

His gaze shifted to me, heavy and merciless. "Do you honestly believe you stumbled upon him by happen-stance? Don't be naïve, Kennedy. Nothing in my world happens by accident."

Cassian stiffened, but Michael still didn't glance his way. He kept his focus locked on me.

"He's here because I made it so. Because I don't leave liabilities unattended. You may call it protection if it helps you sleep, but the truth is simpler: Clearly you needed someone to keep you on a leash so you wouldn't cost me my place in office."

My stomach lurched, twisting on itself until I could barely breathe. The word leash snapped through me, sharp and humiliating. I wasn't his dog to parade or cage, but sitting there, silent, I felt exactly like one.

I turned toward Cassian, desperate for something—denial, explanation, anything that might unravel what Michael had just tied into a noose around my neck. His face gave me nothing. His jaw was clenched tight, his eyes steady on Michael, but not on me. Not once did they flicker back to me.

And that silence... it was worse than any answer he could have given.

My chest burned. Shame pooled hot under my skin, a familiar ache I thought I'd learned to bury. How many times had I been told not to be naïve, not to believe too easily? And here I was again, my heart twisting itself into knots over a man who might have been nothing more than another one of Michael's pieces on the board.

The thought ripped free before I could swallow it back. "So Jaxon and Sienna were right," I whispered, the words breaking apart in my throat. My eyes stung as I searched Cassian's face, desperate and furious all at once. "It was never real."

Cassian's head snapped toward me then, his eyes flashing with something fierce, desperate. "No. Ken—don't say that. You have no idea—"

But my voice cut over his, raw and ragged. "Then tell me what it is. Tell me why I should believe you when everyone else saw the truth but me."

Cassian took a step toward me, but Michael's voice cut in, smooth and final.

"Don't waste your breath, Cassian. She's already starting to see."

His gaze flicked back to me, colder than steel, his words measured like he'd already won. "I'll deal with your little... situation, Kennedy. Quietly. Before it stains my campaign any further."

He didn't wait for an answer. He didn't need one. Michael turned on his heel, his men falling in behind him, and a moment later the door clicked shut—quiet, sharp, final.

The silence after Michael's exit was deafening, his words echoing through me like they'd been carved into stone. *I'll take care of your little... situation.*

I couldn't look at Cassian. Not yet. My pulse roared in my ears, my chest aching with every shallow breath.

Finally, the question ripped free before I could swallow it back.

"Was he lying?" My voice cracked. "Cassian, don't you dare stand there and feed me more bullshit. I want the truth"

His gaze locked on mine, steady, unflinching. When he spoke, his voice was low but razor-sharp, every word deliberate.

"Fine!" He snapped. "No. He wasn't lying. He paid me to keep you contained." His mouth tightened, like the word itself tasted wrong. "Call it managed, watched, handled—whatever makes sense to you. That's how it started. That's the truth."

The floor dropped out from under me. My stomach turned, my skin hot and cold all at once.

"But here's what he didn't tell you." Cassian took a step closer, his voice still calm, still precise, but heavier now, weighted with something raw. "It stopped being about him the moment I met you. I didn't stay because of Michael. I stayed because of you. Because somehow you broke through every line I swore I'd never cross."

The words landed like a blow to my chest, sharp and staggering. My breath caught, breaking in my throat. He said it so simply, so clearly, like it wasn't something dangerous. Like it wasn't something that could undo me all over again.

I wanted to believe him. But Michael's voice still clung to me like poison. My heart wrenched toward Cassian even as my mind screamed to keep my distance.

"How am I supposed to believe you?" My voice trembled, but the bite was still there. "When everything between us—everything—started with lies. Whatever this is, Cassian, it's already poisoned. You made sure of that."

The words cracked between us, sharp and final, and for a heartbeat I wanted them to be the end. To make him feel the same hollow ache splitting through me.

But Cassian didn't flinch. He stepped closer instead, his gaze steady, fierce, unyielding.

"Then hate me for the lies," he said quietly, every syllable deliberate. "But don't you dare doubt my feelings."

The words rang between us, heavy, immovable. My chest tightened, my pulse stuttering against the weight of them.I shook my head, choking on a bitter laugh. "You make it sound so simple. Like I can just... separate one from the other. Like I can pretend this—" I gestured wildly between us, my hands trembling, "—isn't already tainted."

Cassian moved then, slow, deliberate. No sudden reach, no snapping aggression—just a single step closer, then another, until I felt the heat radiating off his body. His presence pressed in, steady and relentless, until my back nearly touched the couch.

"You think I don't know how much I fucked up?" His voice was low, rough, dragging fire through my veins. "You think I don't lie awake at night knowing that I betrayed you? I don't get to rewrite that, Ken. Neither of us do." His jaw flexed, eyes burning into mine. "But I'll be damned if I let it be the thing that breaks us."

My breath hitched, sharp and shaky. I should have shoved him back, should have put distance between us, but instead I stayed rooted to the spot—every nerve alive, every thought tangled.

"You infuriate me," I whispered, though it sounded more like a confession than an accusation.

"Good." His mouth was close now, his breath brushing mine, rough and unsteady. "Hate me. Fight me. Just don't stop feeling for me."

And before I could think better of it, his hand lifted, calloused fingers brushing the side of my jaw, tilting my face up toward him. The contact seared through me, sharp and dangerous.

This time, when his mouth claimed mine, it wasn't soft. It was a collision—rage and desperation sparking into something hotter, wilder, unstoppable.

My mind screamed that it was wrong, that I should shove him away. But my body betrayed me, answering him with equal hunger, equal fury.

Because no matter how poisoned this was—no matter how dangerous—Cassian was the only thing that made me feel alive in the ruin of it all.

Kennedy

14

H is mouth was still on mine when the ache broke through, raw and hollow where my strength should've been. My fingers curled against his chest, not pushing him back, not pulling him closer—just clinging.

"Stop," I breathed, the word fraying in the small space between us. My forehead dropped against his, the plea softer than I meant it to be. "Please… I can't—"

Cassian froze. For a heartbeat, I thought he'd refuse, that he'd drag me right back into the fire. But instead he stilled, his chest heaving against mine. Slowly, carefully, he eased back just enough to give me space, though he didn't let me go entirely.

"I understand," he said quietly, the words rough but steady. No anger. No resistance. Just respect.

The silence stretched, heavy and fragile. My lungs fought to keep rhythm, but my body shook anyway, the tremors small and humiliating against his steady frame.

"I'm so tired," I whispered, almost ashamed to admit it. "Tired of being strong, of pretending I'm not one wrong move away from shattering. I don't even know who I'm fighting anymore—him, you, myself..." My voice cracked, the words dissolving before I could finish.

Cassian's hand moved, tentative, brushing along my arm until his palm covered mine where it fisted against his chest. He pressed my hand there like he was anchoring both of us.

"I'm not your enemy, my Wildfire" he murmured, steady but rough around the edges. "I'm on your side, always."

The words sank into me, sharp and tender all at once, and for a breath I hated how much I wanted to believe them. My chest clenched, the ache spreading hot and cold through every vein.

I wanted the doubt to disappear. I wanted nothing more than to believe his every word. My body leaned into his almost without permission, the steady thrum of his heartbeat under my palm pulling me closer even as my head screamed for distance.

"Cassian..." My voice was raw, torn between fury and longing. "How do I know these aren't just words you're spewing to keep me at bay."

His hand slid to the back of my neck, gentle but unyielding, holding me like I was something fragile he refused to let slip. His forehead brushed mine again, his breath ragged against my lips.

"Give me a chance to show you," he murmured.

The silence that followed stretched taut between us, my pulse hammering so loud I swore he could feel it. His thumb moved slowly against the curve of my jaw, a touch too careful for the man I'd come to know, and that carefulness cut deeper than any plea.

I hated that my body leaned closer still, hated that some part of me craved the steadiness in him like oxygen. The doubt didn't vanish—it pressed sharper, clawing at my ribs—but beneath it was something fiercer, something I couldn't smother no matter how I tried.

Finally, I let out a broken whisper. "Then show me."

Cassian's breath caught, like the words struck him somewhere unguarded. His hand at my neck shifted, cradling instead of holding, his thumb brushing along my skin with a tenderness that felt at odds with the man the world feared.

He didn't kiss me right away. Instead, he searched my face, his green eyes burning, not with fire this time but with something quieter, steadier, like he was memorizing every fracture I'd tried to hide.

The ache in my chest pulled tighter. My body gave before my head could stop it, leaning into the warmth of him, letting his steadiness swallow the tremor in me. When his mouth found mine again, it wasn't the collision of before—it was deliberate, careful, each movement drawn out as if he wanted me to feel the truth in every touch.

My hands, traitorous and trembling, slid up into his shirt, clutching fabric like I needed him to tether me to the ground. His kiss deepened by degrees, patient, giving me every chance to pull away, but I didn't. I couldn't. Because for once, the chaos in my head dulled under the rhythm of him—the press of his lips, the steady thrum of his heartbeat, the way he held me like I was both fragile and unbreakable all at once.

His hands skimmed my sides, slow, careful, as though every curve of me was something he needed to relearn. No urgency, no battle—just patience threaded with hunger he refused to unleash all at once.

"Ken," he breathed against my lips, the syllable more plea than name.

I answered without words, tugging him closer, my body betraying me long before my head could catch up. When his mouth traced lower—to my jaw, my throat—it felt like surrender, and for once I didn't fight it. I let him map the places I'd only ever guarded.

His fingers slipped beneath the hem of my shirt, calloused hands brushing skin in a way that sent shivers scattering down my spine. My breath hitched, ragged, but I didn't pull away. Instead, I arched into him, needing the contact, needing him.

The tenderness of it was almost worse than the fire—like every touch said what words couldn't: I choose you. I love you.

Clothes became an afterthought, tangled between desperate hands and trembling breaths, until the air itself felt charged, thick with everything we hadn't said but were about to show. For once, the fear quieted, the doubts dulled, leaving nothing but him and me and the promise of more.

When he finally entered me, it was slow, reverent, a question asked and answered in the same breath. My gasp caught against his mouth, and his forehead dropped to mine, eyes burning into me like he needed me to feel every ounce of truth in him. I clung tighter, nails biting into his shoulders, body trembling with the ache of finally, finally letting go.

He moved with a rhythm that was steady, unhurried, each thrust a vow. My body rose to meet him, pulled along by a tide I couldn't fight. The chaos that had haunted me for so long quieted beneath him, replaced by something deeper, heavier. This wasn't survival. This was living.

"Ken," he rasped, my name breaking apart on his tongue like a prayer. His hand slid down my thigh, holding me to him, urging me closer, higher.

The storm inside me built with every measured movement, every whispered breath, until the edges of the world blurred. Heat coiled sharp and unbearable, dragging me toward a shatter I couldn't hold back.

And then—

A sharp knock rattled the door.

I froze, the sound slicing through the haze like a blade.

"Shit," Cassian muttered, his voice rough, strained.

Another knock, louder. I scrambled upright, breathless, fumbling for the nearest thing—his shirt. "One second!" I called, too quickly, voice high and unconvincing as I yanked the fabric over my head. The buttons slipped through my fingers, uneven, but it didn't matter. The hem brushed my thighs, swallowing me whole.

Cassian tugged on his pants with a vicious curse, hair tousled, chest still heaving. He glanced at me once, a breathless laugh breaking free, and against my will a shaky giggle bubbled up from my throat. For one ridiculous moment, it felt like we were kids caught sneaking around.

Then he opened the door.

The laugh died instantly.

Sienna stood in the hallway, her face a map of bruises, her lip split, her eyes wide and glassy. Her body swayed, fragile, like one wrong breath would send her crumpling.

The sight hollowed me out, tearing the air from my lungs, leaving only a cold, ringing silence in its place.

My hands clutched at the hem of Cassian's shirt, twisting the fabric as though it could anchor me, as though it could make sense of what I was seeing. But nothing made sense. Not the bruises. Not the way her eyes seemed to beg without words. Not the sudden, gutting reminder that danger wasn't something distant—it was here, breathing down our throats.

"Oh my God… Sienna!"

Kennedy

15

Her name ripped out of me, but it didn't feel like enough. Not when she stood there swaying in the doorway, bruises blooming across her skin like dark fingerprints, her lip split, her eyes wide and unfocused. For a moment my brain refused to connect the girl in front of me with the Sienna I knew—the one who filled every room with noise and laughter, who refused to shrink for anyone. This version of her looked hollowed out. Shaken. Broken.

My legs moved before my mind caught up. I caught her by the arms, her body folding into mine with a weight that felt wrong—too light, too fragile.

"Get her inside," Cassian's voice cut through, sharp and commanding, already reaching past me to slam the door shut. The sound echoed like a gunshot, sealing us in.

I half-dragged, half-guided Sienna across the room, lowering her onto the couch. She sank into the cushions as if her bones had given up. My hands hovered uselessly—touching her hair, her shoulder, pulling back, then reaching again—because nothing I did could fix the damage written all over her face.

Up close, it was worse. One eye was swollen, purple and angry. A bruise trailed along her jaw like someone had tried to erase her smile with their fist. Her hands trembled violently where they clutched the edge of the cushion, knuckles bleached white.

"Oh my God…" My voice cracked as I crouched in front of her. "Sienna, what happened? Who did this to you?"

Her gaze flicked to me, then to Cassian, then back again, skittering like a trapped bird. Her lips parted, but no sound came out. Just a shallow gasp, a tremor running the length of her.

"Breathe," Cassian said, his tone stripped of anything soft, every syllable deliberate. "Start at the beginning."

I shot him a glare, but maybe she needed that steadiness—someone to anchor her while I hovered on the edge of breaking.

Sienna's throat worked as she swallowed, her voice finally scraping out, raw and splintered.

"Jaxon."

The name crashed into me, stealing the air from my lungs. My stomach twisted, sharp and violent, like the floor had given out beneath me.

"No," I whispered, shaking my head even as the bruises on her face screamed otherwise. "No, Sienna… that doesn't make sense. He wouldn't—"

"He would." Her voice cracked on the words, but there was no hesitation. "He did."

Cassian had gone still, arms folded, his gaze narrowed into something unreadable. He didn't speak, didn't move, but the air around him thickened, heavy with a quiet violence I'd come to recognize.

Sienna's hands fisted in the blanket I'd thrown over her lap, knuckles trembling as she clung to the fabric. She pulled in a ragged breath, then another, as if each one cost her more than she had to give.

"I was at his house." Her voice shook, brittle as glass. "He… he always kept one door closed. Said it was just a spare room. I didn't think anything of it—until tonight."

Her gaze darted past me, unfocused, like she was staring at the memory instead of the room we sat in. "I don't even know what made me do it. Curiosity. Stupidity. Whatever it was, I opened the door."

Her whole body shuddered, the words spilling faster now, tumbling over each other. "The walls, Ken… they were covered. Covered in pictures of you. Years of them.

Not just from when you were with him—after. Recent ones. From the café. From your apartment. From places you didn't even know anyone was watching. And it wasn't just pictures." Her throat worked, a sob scraping free. "He had your stuff. Your scarf. A coffee mug. Things that had been *missing*. He kept them like—like trophies."

My breath hitched, my chest caving in as the pieces slammed together. The postcards. The rose. The air-dropped photo from outside my door.

Him.

Cassian finally moved, a muscle ticking hard along his jaw. "And he caught you."

Sienna flinched at the sound of his voice but nodded, tears spilling hot down her bruised cheeks. "I didn't even hear him coming until it was too late. He—" Her hand drifted to her swollen lip, her voice breaking. "He lost it. Said I ruined everything. Said I wasn't supposed to see. And then he... he hit me. Over and over. I thought—" Her voice fractured, dissolving into a ragged sob. "I thought he was going to kill me."

I reached for her hands, gripping them tight, my own shaking just as violently. "But you got out. You're here—you got away."

She nodded, breath stuttering. "Barely. I don't even remember how I made it to my car. I just drove. I didn't know where else to go, and then I remembered that you share your location with me. I saw you were here."

Her words collapsed into silence, heavy and suffocating. My heart thundered against my ribs, each beat sharp and uneven, as if it might tear itself apart from the inside.

I wanted to scream. To cry. To break apart. But I couldn't—not when Sienna was in pieces right in front of me.

Cassian stepped closer, his shadow falling over both of us, his voice low but edged like a blade. "He's escalating."

I lifted my gaze, meeting the storm in his eyes. He wasn't asking. He was stating a fact. A deadly one.

Her head bowed, hair falling forward to shield her face, her shoulders shaking. At first I thought it was just the pain, another tremor rattling through her body—but then I heard it.

"I'm sorry." Her voice was barely a whisper, cracked and broken, but it sliced straight through me.

I shook my head quickly. "Don't. You don't have anything to—"

"I do," she rasped, cutting me off. Her eyes brimmed, spilling over as her face crumpled.

"God, Ken, I was so wrong. About him. About everything. I should have listened, I should have believed you, I should have—" Her words dissolved into a sob. "I defended him. I let myself believe he was different. And all this time…"

She broke off, clutching the blanket desperately.. "I'm sorry for the fight. I'm sorry for the things I said. I'm sorry I didn't see it…"

My chest tightened so painfully I thought it might split. I hadn't been thinking about our fight. Not once. All I could see was the damage carved into her face, the fear in her eyes.

I reached for her again, wrapping my arms around her shaking frame. "Sienna, stop. None of that matters right now. You're here. You're safe. That's all I care about."

She let out a strangled sob against my shoulder, clinging to me with a desperation that scraped me raw.

Cassian stood off to the side, silent, watchful, his expression unreadable. But I caught the way his jaw worked, the way his hands flexed once at his sides, like he wanted to tear the world apart piece by piece.

For a moment we embraced each other while Cassian gave us the space we needed to console one another. As I pulled away I took another look at my best friend and I couldn't stand to look at her face another second without doing something—anything. I shot up and headed for the kitchen, my hands moving before my brain caught up. The freezer door banged open, and I grabbed the first thing I saw—a half-empty bag of frozen peas, hard and lumpy under my fingers.

"Here," I said, pressing it gently into her hands when I came back. "Hold this to your face."

She let out a shaky laugh, the sound collapsing into a wince as the movement tugged at her split lip. "Peas? Really?"

"For the swelling." My throat was too tight for anything more.

She lifted the bag and pressed it against her cheek anyway, closing her eyes as though the cold anchored her back in her body.

Cassian stayed silent, his posture coiled and deliberate, but I could feel the storm simmering off him. He leaned against the wall, arms crossed, eyes sharp and unblinking as he watched every twitch of Sienna's expression, every stumble in her story.

"Where is he now?" Cassian asked finally.

Her eyes flicked open, wide and frightened. "I don't know. I didn't look back. I just drove."

"Did he follow you?"

"I—I don't think so. But I can't…" Her voice broke as her gaze darted to me again. "Ken, I can't go back there. I can't even—"

"You're not," I cut in quickly, maybe too quickly. "You're staying here tonight."

Cassian's stare sharpened, his jaw flexing as he pushed off the wall. "Both of you—turn off your phone locations. Now."

Sienna blinked at him, confused. "What?"

"You said you found her because of location sharing," he said flatly. "If you can see her, then he can too. If Jaxon got into your phone, if he hacked anything, if he's tracking you in ways you don't even realize—" He cut himself off with a sharp shake of his head. "I won't risk it. Shut it off."

My stomach sank. It hadn't even occurred to me. I fumbled for my phone, thumb shaking as I dove through the settings. Beside me, Sienna moved slower, her bruised fingers clumsy as she followed.

Cassian's gaze stayed locked on us until we'd both done it, his presence like iron in the room. When he finally leaned back again, his voice dropped lower, more dangerous. "That's one less tether for him to use."

Her lips trembled, another tear streaking down through the swelling. For once, she didn't argue. She just nodded, clutching the peas tighter against her bruised face.

I sank back onto the couch beside her, tucking my knees up under me, trying to keep my hands from shaking. I wanted to believe we were safe here—that the walls around us and Cassian's presence were enough. But the dread in my chest told me otherwise.

Sienna sunk back into the cushions, exhaustion pulling at her face until she looked smaller than I'd ever seen her. The peas slipped a little, sliding against her cheek, but she didn't have the strength to readjust.

I took them gently from her hand, held them in place myself, and brushed her hair back from her face. "We'll figure this out tomorrow," I whispered, even though tomorrow felt like a cliff I couldn't see over. "Right now, you just need to rest."

Her eyes fluttered shut, a tear sliding down into her hairline, and for once she didn't argue, didn't fight.

Cassian crossed the room and dropped onto the opposite end of the couch, his presence filling the space like a wall. He didn't touch her, didn't look at me, but I could feel the promise radiating off him—if Jaxon showed up tonight, he'd never make it out alive.

There was no way I was leaving Sienna alone, not in this state. So I pulled a blanket from the armchair and curled up beside her. Cassian stayed where he was, silent and steady, like a guard posted for the night.

The three of us sat there in the dim light of the living room, the city humming faintly outside, the air thick with dread. We weren't safe, not really. But for this one fragile night, we were together.

Morning came too soon. I woke with a crick in my neck and a blanket tangled around my legs, the faint hum of the city bleeding in through the windows. Sienna was still beside me, her head tilted toward the cushions, her breath shallow but steady. Cassian was exactly where he'd been when I closed my eyes—seated in the armchair, one ankle crossed over a knee, his eyes trained on the door like he hadn't blinked all night.

For a moment, I let myself believe in the silence. That the world hadn't shifted, that last night was just a nightmare we'd managed to outlast.

But then Sienna stirred, the bruises standing out in the gray light, and reality returned like a punch to the ribs.

"Hey," I whispered, brushing a strand of hair from her face. "How are you feeling?"

"Like I got hit by a truck." Her voice was rough, but there was a faint spark of humor beneath it. The kind that made my throat tighten, because even broken, she was still Sienna.

Cassian stood, stretching once before moving toward the kitchen. "I'll make coffee."

A laugh slipped out of me before I could stop it—hoarse, but real. "You do realize I own a coffee shop, right? I'm the barista here."

He paused, glancing back at me with one brow raised. "And yet, you look half-dead on that couch. Let me do it."

Sienna let out the faintest laugh, muffled under the blanket. "He's got a point."

I shook my head, but the corner of my mouth tugged upward despite everything. For once, Sienna and Cassian were in the same room without sharp words or ugly looks between them. No tension. No competition. Just... us. And it felt almost natural, like maybe this fragile bubble could hold a little longer.

Hours slipped by in fragments—coffee mugs half-empty on the table, Sienna drifting in and out of sleep, Cassian pacing like a storm contained by four walls. For the first time since last night, the air almost felt breathable again.

Until my phone rang.

The sound sliced through the quiet, too sharp, too sudden. For a second, I thought about ignoring it—pretending it didn't exist, pretending I could stay in this small pocket of calm—but something in my chest said *don't*.

Sienna glanced up from the couch, her brows knitting. "Who is it?"

"Izzy," I said, already swiping to answer.

Her voice came out in pieces, shaking, like she was trying to talk through tears or fear—or both. "K-Kennedy?"

My stomach dropped. "Izzy, what's wrong?"

There was noise in the background. Muffled. A crash, maybe? Or movement? Her breath hitched. "I—I can't—"

"Izzy?"

Cassian's head snapped up from across the room, his eyes finding mine. He mouthed, *What is it?*

"Izzy, talk to me," I said, standing now, pacing toward the door even though I had no idea where I thought I was going. "Where are you?"

Her voice was barely audible. "The café." And then silence.

"Izzy?" Nothing. Dead air.

Sienna stood up slowly, her face drained of color. "The café? She—the cafes closed though?"

Cassian was already on his feet, jaw tight, all composure gone. "What happened?"

"I don't know. She sounded terrified." My hand shook as I grabbed my keys.

Cassian stepped closer. "You're not going alone."

Sienna blinked at him, dazed. "Then I'm going with her."

"Absolutely not," Cassian said, his tone final.

"Cassian—"

He cut me off, voice hard. "You don't know what you're walking into. If he's there—"

"If he's there," I snapped, "then it's already too late!"

He flinched, but didn't move. I could see the battle behind his eyes—the need to control colliding with the need to protect.

"I can't just sit here," I said. My voice cracked, my chest burning. "I can't."

His jaw flexed. Then quieter, "You're not going without me."

"I don't need your permission," I shot back. "You've done enough pretending it's about protecting me."

Something flickered across his face. Regret. Maybe pain. I didn't wait to find out which.

Sienna was already moving toward the door. "Then let's go."

I grabbed my coat and followed her out before I could lose my nerve. The door slammed behind us, the sound echoing down the hall.

The air outside hit me like ice.

My pulse was too loud in my ears, too heavy in my chest. Every step toward the car felt mechanical—keys, ignition, drive.

The drive over felt heavier than it should have. The streets were quiet, sunlight stretched across the pavement. The café wasn't far, but the closer I got, the worse the dread crawled up my spine. Something in my gut already knew I was too late.

I spotted Izzy's car first—parked crooked near the curb, driver's door hanging open. My hands shook as I threw mine into park.

The café should've looked harmless, familiar. Instead, it felt wrong—like the air around it had shifted, holding its breath.

I pushed the door open, the faint jingle of the bell overhead slicing through the silence. My chest tightened at the sound. It should've been comforting. It wasn't. It felt different. Too quiet. Too still. A chair tipped on its side, a mug shattered near the counter, coffee bleeding across the tile.

"Stay up front," I told Sienna, forcing steadiness into my voice. "Keep an eye on the doors. "

Sienna nodded, straightening her posture by the registers even though her bruised face betrayed her exhaustion.

The café smelled the same—coffee beans and vanilla syrup lingering in the air—but underneath it was something faint, something metallic that didn't belong. I moved slowly past the tables, each step too loud against the floor.

"Izzy?" My voice echoed off the walls, swallowed by silence.

I reached the swinging door that led to the back and pushed it open, my pulse hammering in my throat. The storage room was dim, the overhead light flickering weakly, boxes stacked high along the shelves.

A scream tore out of me before I could stop it.

There she was, lying crumpled on the floor, her body slack, her chest rising in shallow, uneven breaths.

"Izzy!" Her name escaped my lips as I dropped to my knees, reaching for her shoulder, shaking her lightly. "Oh my God—Izzy, can you hear me?"

Her eyelids fluttered, a groan slipping past her lips, but she didn't wake.

Relief crashed into panic, colliding in my chest. I was so focused on her that I almost missed it—the soft scuff of a shoe behind me, the shift of air that meant I wasn't alone.

I froze.

Before I could turn, a hand clamped over my mouth, rough and unrelenting. My scream died against his palm as an arm locked around my waist, yanking me back.

The world spun in a blur of shadows and shelves, my heels scraping uselessly against the floor as I thrashed. A box toppled off the rack, slamming to the ground with a deafening crash—

Kennedy

16

Cold. That was the first thing I felt. A damp chill seeping up from the floor, curling around my ankles, clawing through my clothes until it sank into my bones.

My head throbbed with every beat of my heart, heavy and unsteady. When I tried to move, ropes bit into my wrists, pinning them tight behind the back of the chair. Each twist scraped my skin raw.

I sucked in a breath too sharp, chest jerking. The air reeked faintly of mildew, dust, and something metallic. A single bulb buzzed overhead, flickering just enough to make the shadows twitch on the walls.

It took a moment before the space stopped tilting, before my vision steadied. Concrete. Low ceiling. A doorway braced with heavy wood.

Something about it clawed at my memory, sharp and buried.

No.

I blinked, harder, dragging in another breath that burned all the way down. The crack in the wall by the corner—the one shaped like a crooked lightning bolt. The rusted shelving unit sagging against the far side.

Recognition sliced through the haze, colder than the air.

I knew this place.

The bunker. The one Sienna and I had stumbled on in the woods when we were kids, half-daring each other to go inside, half-terrified of what we might find. Later it became something else—our secret escape, a place to drink warm beer, gossip, throw parties that felt bigger than they actually were.

Other memories bled in, sharper, harder to push back. The taste of stolen vodka. Music rattling off the concrete. Fingers laced with mine in the dark. Laughter pressed close against my ear.

Jaxon.

My stomach knotted. Of course he'd bring me here. Of course he'd twist a place that once belonged to *us* into something I could never escape. He hadn't just taken me. He'd dragged me back to where it all started.

Jaxon stepped into the weak circle of light, and for a second my brain refused to connect him to the boy I used to know. His hair clung damp to his forehead, his skin pale and waxy like he hadn't slept in days. Shadows bruised the skin beneath his eyes, hollowing his face until he looked almost skeletal.

I'd seen him angry before. Tired. Even drunk. But this—this was something else entirely. His movements were too sharp, his eyes too wide, glinting with a feverish brightness that made him almost unrecognizable.

The silence dragged, and it was worse than shouting. He just stood there, watching me, his chest rising and falling like every breath cost him something. The Jaxon I remembered—the one who kissed me in the dark corners of this place, who whispered promises against my skin—wasn't in front of me anymore.

This man was a stranger wearing his face.

My pulse hammered, loud in my ears. I opened my mouth, but nothing came out.

And then he smiled.

It was wrong. Twisted. A jagged edge of something I'd never seen in him before.

"Oh good, you're awake!" He finally said, his voice scraping the silence apart.

He stepped closer under the flickering light, and I caught the twitch in his jaw, the way his hands flexed like he couldn't keep them still. Every line of him screamed exhaustion—like he hadn't slept in days—but underneath was something more. Feverish.

I swallowed, my throat dry and aching. "Jaxon…" My voice barely made it out, cracked and trembling.

His head tilted, just slightly, eyes catching on mine with a brightness that made my skin crawl. "God, I almost thought you wouldn't wake up. Would've been a shame, after all the trouble I went through to get you here."

My stomach twisted. "Where—why am I—" The ropes bit deeper into my wrists as I shifted.

His laugh snapped out, too sharp, too sudden, echoing off the concrete like it didn't belong to just one man. But there was no humor in it. His smile cut away as fast as it came, replaced by something darker.

"You don't recognize it?" His voice dropped, incredulous, laced with fury. He took a step closer, the shadows stretching long behind him. "Don't insult me, Kennedy. Don't insult *us.*"

My chest tightened.

His mouth twitched, splitting into a grin again, but it didn't reach his eyes. "Our place."

The words hit like ice water down my spine. I'd recognized it already, deep down, but hearing him spit it out—hearing the *anger* behind it—made bile rise in my throat.

This wasn't nostalgia. It was possession.

His grin faltered, the twitch returning at the corner of his mouth. "You should've known the second you opened your eyes." His voice cracked sharp, rising too fast. "This place was ours, Kennedy. That's not something you just forget."

He started pacing, the scrape of his shoes harsh against the concrete, too quick, too restless. His fingers raked through his hair, tugging hard enough to make him wince, and then he swung back toward me with that same wild brightness in his eyes.

"You, me, Sienna—we built everything here. This is where you said you'd always come back to me. Remember?" His smile twisted, bitter and triumphant all at once. "And look at that. You did."

The ropes cut into my skin as I pulled back as far as I could, the chair groaning under me. My stomach churned. I wanted to scream that I'd never promised him forever, that teenage words and stolen kisses didn't mean this—but I couldn't force the air out.

Because for the first time, I realized Jaxon didn't just want me here.

He believed I *belonged* here.

"You shouldn't have fought it," Jaxon said, his voice dropping low, almost coaxing. He moved behind me, his footsteps slow, deliberate, the scrape of his shoes on concrete raising every hair on my neck. "You think I don't see it? The way you look at me when you think no one's watching?"

I shook my head, too fast. "You're wrong—"

"Wrong?" His laugh broke sharp again, ricocheting off the walls. He leaned down close enough that his breath brushed my ear. "I've never been wrong about you, Kennedy. Not once."

My pulse thundered. The ropes dug deeper into my skin, but it didn't matter—I couldn't move anyway. My body was locked, braced for whatever came next.

He straightened suddenly, pacing again, running a hand over his face like he could rub the frenzy out of himself. When he looked back, his smile was gone. His eyes were hollow, dark.

"You never should've been fine without me."

The words cut sharper than any shout. Jaxon stood still now, staring at me like I was something that had betrayed him.

"I let you go," he said, almost softly, but his hands curled into fists. "I'm the one that ended it. And you—you were supposed to fall apart. You were supposed to *need* me." His voice cracked, the quiet unraveling into a rasp. "But you didn't. You laughed and lived your life. You built this whole little world like I never even mattered."

My breath stuttered.

His face twisted, pale skin stretched tight over the fury burning underneath. "Do you know what it was like? Watching you walk around like you were whole, like you were happy without me? Like I was disposable?" He took a step closer, too close. "That's when I knew. You needed reminding. You needed to be reminded that you've always been mine."

The ropes dug deeper into my wrists as I tried to pull back, but there was nowhere to go. His eyes shone wild in the flickering light, feverish, broken.

"You never should've let him get so close."

My breath caught. Him. He didn't have to say a name—I knew who he meant. Cassian.

"You think he can protect you." Jaxon's voice rose, cracking on the edges. He slammed his palm against the wall, the sound booming through the bunker, making me flinch. "He doesn't know you like I do. He doesn't *love* you like I do. He was supposed to be nothing. And you—" His chest heaved, wild, ragged. "You're mine."

The bulb overhead buzzed angrily before settling again, shadows jittering with every movement, stretching long and monstrous across the walls.

My lungs seized, panic clawing higher, but I forced the air down, forcing myself to steady against the ropes. Cassian's voice came back to me, low and certain, from nights when fear had nearly swallowed me whole.

You will not break.

I lifted my chin, even as my wrists burned raw against the ropes. My voice shook, but it came out steady enough to sting. "I didn't choose him *over* you, Jaxon. I chose him because he's good. Because he's not you."

His face twisted, the fever-bright fury in his eyes flashing hotter.

"He knows me," I pressed on, pulse racing, words tumbling before I could lose my nerve. "He sees me. All of me. And no matter what you do, no matter where you drag me, you can't take that away."

For a heartbeat, silence crashed over us, thick and suffocating. His chest rose and fell, ragged, and the twitch in his jaw deepened.

Then he laughed—sharp, broken, a sound that made the walls vibrate.

But when it cut off, the cold in his eyes froze me to the chair.

He turned, slow and deliberate, toward the battered shelving against the wall. Metal scraped as he dragged something free. The bulb flickered again, throwing the object in and out of shadow until it gleamed. A knife.

My pulse slammed so hard it hurt.

Jaxon held it loosely at first, running his thumb along the flat of the blade, his expression unreadable. Then he lifted it, letting the tip hover under my chin. Just enough pressure that I could feel the sting.

His voice was quiet now, stripped of frenzy, almost tender.

"I'd rather see you bleed than watch you love him."

The words wrapped tighter than the ropes on my wrists, squeezing the air from my lungs.

I forced myself to stay still, to keep my chin from trembling against the blade. Cassian's voice surged through me, steady, unyielding.

You will not break.

I swallowed hard, tasting copper. I would not give Jaxon the satisfaction of seeing me crumble. Not now. Not ever.

The knife pressed harder, just enough to make the skin on my throat sting. My wrists burned raw against the ropes, but I forced myself still. He wanted me to tremble. He wanted me to crack.

Instead, I met his eyes.

"You hate him," I rasped, my voice shredded but steady. "Because you'll never be him. He doesn't have to beg. He doesn't have to trap me to keep me close."

For a second, something flickered across Jaxon's face—shock, almost hurt. Then his mouth twisted, pulling into a snarl. The hand holding the knife trembled, the tip digging harder into my skin until I could feel the bead of blood gathering there.

"You think he's better than me?" His voice cracked, too high, too raw. "You think he's different?" He barked out a laugh that sounded nothing like him, bouncing harsh off the bunker walls. "God, you really don't have a clue, do you?"

He leaned closer until his forehead almost brushed mine, the stink of sleeplessness and sweat clinging to him. His words hissed through clenched teeth.

"You don't even know what he is. What he does for a living."

The bottom dropped out of my stomach. My heart lurched so hard it hurt. The words didn't make sense—not fully—but there was weight behind them, heavy and jagged, like they'd been rotting in him for a long time.

"What—" My voice cracked, raw with panic. "What are you talking about?"

Jaxon's grin returned, but it was hollow, stretched too wide. His eyes gleamed fever-bright as he dragged the knife down, the blade grazing from the hollow of my throat to the ropes at my wrists, deliberate, taunting.

"You think he's your happily ever after," Jaxon murmured, voice low and shaking with something that wasn't quite laughter. "Oh sweet Kennedy, he's your grim reaper."

The words landed like a blade in my chest, sharper than the one grazing my skin. My pulse thundered, my breath choking against my ribs. I yanked against the ropes without meaning to, the fibers slicing deeper into my wrists, but there was no give.

He watched me struggle, head tilted, his expression caught between amusement and reverence, like he was seeing exactly what he wanted. The knife twitched in his grip, catching the weak bulb's flicker until it gleamed bright, hungry.

Then his smile thinned into something colder. His voice softened, steady, certain.

"You've been running on borrowed time, Kennedy."

The words settled heavy in my chest, pressing tighter than the ropes cutting into my wrists. My pulse slammed against the blade's edge, the air thinning around me until every breath scraped.

Jaxon's grin didn't widen this time. It thinned, cold and final, like he'd already decided how this would end.

Cassian

17

I paced. Back and forth, each step dragging against the weight in my chest. My body wanted motion—wanted to follow her, track her, keep her in sight—but all I had was the silence.

Respect her wishes. That's what I'd promised myself. That's what she'd asked of me. Let her make her own choices. Let her breathe.

My fists curled anyway.

Minutes bled into each other, stretching thin. The city glittered beneath the glass, a hundred thousand lights burning like they knew something I didn't. Every one of them mocked me. Out there, anything could happen. Out there, she was—

I forced my jaw to unclench.

She wasn't fragile. She wasn't helpless. She was fire. Wildfire.

But fire burned out if you didn't protect it.

I dragged a hand over my face, pushing back the storm rising inside me. If I followed her too soon, it would prove her right—that I couldn't trust her to handle herself. But if I didn't— Every second she was gone, that restraint felt more like a mistake.

Every second dragged like glass in my veins.

I told myself it was fine. She'd text when it was done. She'd laugh at me later for pacing a hole in the floor. And I'd let her. Because she was right—I couldn't keep treating her like she was fragile. She wasn't.

Still—

Something was off.

I crossed to the window, scanning the sprawl of the city lights, but the answer wasn't out there. It was in the silence itself. Too deep. Too long.

My gut clenched hard. That instinct—the one that had saved my skin more times than I could count—screamed at me now.

Kennedy wasn't fine.

I didn't remember grabbing my jacket or the keys, just the slam of the door behind me. The elevator took forever. My reflection in the metal doors looked foreign—jaw clenched, eyes hollow, the shadow of what

I used to be. I tried to steady my breathing. Failed. By the time the doors opened, I was already moving, already half-running through the dimly lit garage.

The air outside hit hard and cold, scraping against my skin. It smelled like exhaust and rain. The kind of night where the city hummed with electricity and secrets.

The drive started smooth, too quiet. The kind of quiet that makes you suspicious. I caught every red light, every slow turn, every damn reason the world could think of to keep me from getting where I needed to be.

Three blocks from downtown, the traffic stopped dead.

A wall of brake lights bled across the road in front of me, each one pulsing in time with the pounding in my head. Engines idled. Horns blared. No one moved.

I gripped the steering wheel until my knuckles ached. My pulse thudded against my teeth.

Thirty seconds. A minute. Two.

Every one of them, a chance for something to go wrong.

I checked my phone. Nothing. Not a call. Not a text.

She was out there, and I was here—boxed in, staring at a sea of cars that weren't going anywhere.

The longer I sat there, the smaller the car felt. The dashboard lights blurred. My breathing went shallow. I could feel the edges of that old panic pressing in—the one I thought I'd buried years ago.

I hit the steering wheel once, the sound sharp in the silence. Then again. Harder.

A horn answered me from somewhere ahead. Someone yelled. It didn't matter. The city didn't care.

And then—sirens.

Faint, buried under the noise at first. Then closer. Rising.

I turned my head, searching for the source, the reflection of lights bouncing off glass and steel. Ambulance. Then another. Police.

They came from the opposite end of the street, cutting through traffic like a blade. Every car around me began shifting, one by one, moving aside.

That's when I saw it—an opening. A thin strip of space between bumpers, just wide enough.

I took it.

The car jolted as I swerved into the gap, following in the wake of the emergency vehicles. The sirens screamed ahead of me, echoing down the corridor of buildings like a warning I was too slow to understand.

At first, I didn't know where they were headed. Then, a turn. Southbound.

My stomach dropped. South was the café.

My chest constricted, a vice tightening with every streetlight that passed. I tried to tell myself it was a coincidence. Random. Anything. But every second I drove, that hope unraveled a little more.

The closer I got, the worse it felt. The noise grew louder, the air thicker. The traffic thinned—people were pulling over, watching, whispering.

And then I saw the reflection of flashing lights bouncing off the windows ahead.

No.

By the time I turned the corner onto Third, I already knew.

Red and blue lights strobed against the glass of the café, spilling across the pavement. The sirens hadn't even died yet—one screamed past me as I pulled up, brakes shrieking, lights still spinning. Paramedics were already spilling out of the back of the ambulance, hauling gear. Two squad cars pulled in behind them, tires spitting water, doors slamming.

I shoved the car into park and was out before the engine stopped. The door was open before my brain could catch up. Cold air hit, sharp and metallic, thick with exhaust and adrenaline. Boots hit the pavement hard. The noise around me blurred—radios crackling, voices shouting orders I couldn't make out.

Someone yelled, "Sir, you can't—"

I didn't stop. Didn't look.

I was already moving—shoulder-checking past a cop trying to get the perimeter started, ducking under an arm that wasn't there a second ago.

The bell above the door gave a sharp jingle as I shoved it open, but the sound vanished under the chaos inside—voices barking orders, radios spitting static, EMTs crowding around a stretcher.

I didn't stop. I cut straight through the noise, every stride pushing back against the red-and-blue glare bleeding through the windows. My eyes swept the scene once, fast and precise—the scuff marks across the tile, the boxes knocked off their shelves, Izzy strapped to a gurney with an oxygen mask fogging faintly over her face.

But none of that mattered.

Sienna stood near the counter, pale under the harsh lights, her bruises darker now against her skin. She looked like she was barely holding herself upright. My gut clenched.

"What happened?" My voice carried, rough enough to cut through the chatter. "Where's Kennedy?"

I closed the distance in long, quick strides, scanning again, searching for anything—blood, a sign, a shadow. My chest was already tight, but when Sienna's eyes met mine, raw and red-rimmed, I knew before she spoke.

"She's gone." Her whisper cracked in the middle, shredding what was left of my composure. "Kennedy's gone."

I froze. The air in the room seemed to thin, every sound distant, unimportant. Then the heat roared back, fast and violent.

"What the fuck do you mean she's gone?" My voice snapped like a whip, too loud, too sharp. Heads turned. Cops stared. I didn't care.

I surged closer before I could stop myself, the rage burning hotter than the fear in my chest. Sienna flinched back, her shoulders jerking tight. For a flash, the look on her face twisted my gut—she wasn't seeing me. She was seeing him.

Jaxon.

I forced myself to stop short, fists curling so tight my knuckles ached. My anger wasn't for her. It was for him. For the space he'd ripped Kennedy out of. For daring to touch her.

Still, the sight of Sienna's fear lodged like a blade under my ribs. I'd never let myself lose that kind of control in front of her before. Now she'd seen the edge of it.

A detective cleared his throat, trying to seize the moment back. "And you are?"

"Cassian Drake." My voice was clipped, vibrating with restraint I barely held onto.

"Relation to the victim?"

My answer came quiet, but it cut like glass. "Close."

The detective frowned, unimpressed. "Mr. Drake, this is an active investigation. If you'd wait outside—"

My head snapped toward him, whipcrack fast. The rookie nearest us shifted again, uneasy. I stepped closer, my voice edged to cut through the noise.

"Fine," I bit out. "But she's coming with me."

The detective's frown deepened, his pen hovering over the page. "The woman stays. She's still giving her statement."

I turned my gaze on Sienna, then back on him. My voice dropped, low and dangerous.

"She's given enough. She knows Kennedy. She knows Jaxon. You want me to wait outside while you shuffle papers and trip over your own procedures?" My jaw locked. "Or you can let me take the only person who might actually help me bring her back before it's too late."

The detective stiffened, jaw tightening. He stepped forward like he thought he could hold the line. "Mr. Drake, if you interfere—"

I leaned in just enough for him to feel the weight of it, the fury rolling off me sharp as steel. "I'm not interfering," I said, teeth flashing in something that wasn't a smile. "I'm going to find her."

The cool air pressed against me as I pushed through the café doors, Sienna trailing a half-step behind. The noise of cops and medics cut off with the slam of the door, sirens muffled to a hum outside. Out here, the air was quieter—too quiet—but it sharpened everything inside me.

Kennedy. Gone.

The word pulsed through me like a second heartbeat. I forced my breathing slow. Panic blurred edges. I couldn't afford that. Not now.

Sienna's arms wrapped tight across her chest as she followed me toward the car. She looked small in the yellow wash of the streetlamp, bruises stark against her skin. She didn't say a word, but her silence was loud—fear, guilt, grief, all of it clinging to her in waves.

I opened the passenger door. She slid in without protest. Good.

The drive back cut through the city in a blur of neon and shadow. I kept my hands steady on the wheel, eyes cutting between headlights and mirrors, tracking every movement on the streets around us. Sienna sat rigid beside me, glancing at me once or twice like she wanted to say something but thought better of it.

Smart. Words are useless right now.

The penthouse loomed up out of the dark—glass, steel, sharp lines, order. I swiped us inside, the elevator carrying us up in silence. Sienna hugged herself tighter, her reflection pale against the chrome walls.

When the doors slid open, she lingered just inside, arms crossed like she wasn't sure if she wanted to come any farther. The space was the same to the eye—clean lines, quiet, the city sprawling wide beneath the glass—but the atmosphere felt stripped bare. Empty.

I wondered if she felt it too, the hollow in the air where Kennedy should've been.

She stepped in finally, her boots soft against the polished floor, her gaze flicking over the space like she was cataloguing details she'd already seen before. I didn't ask what she thought. I didn't care.

Her hesitation dragged for a beat too long, but I didn't wait for her. My legs carried me through the quiet, each step echoing harder in the hollow air. Straight down the hall, past the living room, past the view of the city—none of it mattered.

What mattered was behind a locked panel recessed into the wall.

My code punched in smooth, muscle memory, the quiet click of gears unlocking almost soothing. The door swung open to reveal steel and black matte—rows of weapons, ammunition, blades lined with perfect order.

I pulled the case open, fingers brushing the hilt of the knife I knew best. The weight slid into my palm like it belonged there.

Behind me, Sienna's footsteps faltered.

"You've got to be kidding me," she whispered, her voice frayed, barely more than breath.

I didn't turn. The Glock came next, slide checked, magazine slammed home with a sound that cut through the room. The gun hit the counter beside the knife with a solid, deliberate thud.

"Cassian…" her voice cracked, thin and raw. "What the hell is this?"

"Preparation," I said. No hesitation. No room for argument.

"For what?" Her words splintered, tight with fear.

I finally looked at her. Her arms were locked across her ribs, shoulders rigid, eyes wide but burning. Bruises colored her face, her skin too pale against them. She looked like she might shatter, but her jaw held tight, clenched against it.

"We're bringing her home." The words came flat, clipped, final. I loaded another magazine, each metallic snap dragging the silence tighter. "So think. Hard. Where would he have taken her?"

Her silence stretched, the air between us pulled thin. She shook her head, frustrated. "I don't know." Her arms wrapped tighter across her ribs, her voice climbing, brittle. "He could've taken her anywhere."

"Not just anywhere, Sienna" My tone cut sharp. "Somewhere that's special to him, a safe place. Maybe a place where they share a memory?"

She flinched, eyes squeezing shut. I could almost see the memories turning behind them, ugly and unwelcome.

When she spoke again, it was quieter. "I know a place…it's been so long I almost forgot it existed." Her throat bobbed. "Back in high school. Out past the woods." She hesitated, biting hard at her lip. "There's this bunker Kennedy and I found during our freshman year. We all used to hang out there—me, Kennedy, Jaxon. Drinking, messing around. Jaxon even lost his vir-"

The words tripped over her tongue, halting sharp when she caught the flicker in my eyes. I didn't move, didn't say a word. Just one brow raised, slow and deliberate — enough of a warning to remind her she was about to step somewhere she shouldn't.

Her throat worked, and she backpedaled fast. "After a while it was only a spot for them. Their... special place."

I loaded the last magazine with a snap, the sound jagged in the silence. The knot in my chest tightened. I hung onto the words "special place". Of course he'd take her back there.

Holstering the Glock. My voice came out low, final. "Lead the way."

Sienna's directions guided us out of the city, the skyline shrinking in the rearview until it was nothing but a smear of steel and light swallowed by the dark. The farther we drove, the thinner the traffic became, the quieter the world turned. Asphalt gave way to cracked roads and dirt shoulders, streetlights vanishing until the headlights carved the only path forward.

She sat rigid in the passenger seat, arms locked tight across her chest, jaw clenched hard. Every so often, her gaze flicked toward me like she wanted to argue, to say something, but she swallowed it down. Good. Silence was better.

When the woods finally closed in on either side of us, her voice came rough, almost unwilling. "Turn here."

I swung the wheel, tires crunching over gravel. The road narrowed, swallowed by trees that stretched tall and black against the night sky. Branches clawed at the car as we pushed deeper, the headlights bouncing off trunks, throwing warped shadows across the ground.

"This is it," Sienna said finally, but her voice was too quiet, too brittle.

I braked hard, the car shuddering to a stop on uneven ground. The woods stretched ahead, thick and dark, the faint outline of a trail cutting through them. Beyond that trail—I already knew.

My hands curled on the wheel once before I shut off the engine. The silence that followed pressed heavy, thick enough to choke on.

I turned to her. "You're staying here."

Her head snapped toward me, eyes wide. "What? No. I'm not just sitting in the car while—"

"Yes. You are." My voice cut clean, no room for debate. "If he's in there, it's not safe. Not for you."

Her breath hitched, and she shook her head, stubborn, desperate. "Cassian, I can help—"

"You've helped enough." My words came out sharper than I meant, but I didn't pull them back. She needed to hear them. "You told me where he took her. That's all I needed. Now you stay put. If anything comes at you, you drive. Don't wait, don't argue—go."

Her throat bobbed, her hands gripping the seatbelt strap like she might tear it off. "And what about you?"

I slid the Glock from its holster, racking the slide with a clean, deliberate motion. "I'll handle it."

For a beat, she just stared at me, breathing shallow, caught somewhere between anger and fear. Then, finally, she sank back into the seat, her fists tightening in her lap. "You better bring her back," she muttered, voice cracked but steady.

I didn't answer. I just stepped out.

The cold hit me first—sharp, damp, laced with the bite of earth and rot. The door shut behind me, sealing Sienna into the fragile safety of the car. Out here, there was only the crunch of gravel under my boots and the whisper of wind dragging through the branches.

I moved fast, steady, following the faint scar of a trail through the trees. Every sense sharpened, tuned for movement, sound, threat. The woods pressed close on either side, shadows layered on shadows, the dark swallowing everything but the narrow reach of the flashlight clipped to my belt.

Minutes bled into each other, the path winding deeper. Then, through the trees, the outline emerged.

Concrete, half-buried in earth and weeds. The bunker.

It sat hunched in the clearing like a secret the world had tried to forget—edges crumbling, the steel door streaked with rust, graffiti faded across the walls. The air here was different—colder, heavier, tinged with mildew and something older, like the place had been waiting.

My jaw tightened. Of course he'd bring her here.

I slowed, scanning the ground—tire tracks pressed shallow in the dirt, footprints trailing toward the door. Fresh.

The knot in my chest cinched tighter.

I adjusted my grip on the Glock, the weight familiar, steady in my hand. My body shifted into that old rhythm—silent steps, measured breaths, every nerve pulled taut and ready.

Kennedy was in there.

I felt it.

And no matter what waited between us, I was getting her out.

Kennedy

18

The knife hadn't left my skin. Every breath dragged me closer to the edge, shallow and burning, like my own body was betraying me. The steel was cold, but the place it touched seemed to sear into me, branding me with its threat.

Jaxon's eyes stayed fixed on mine, wide and fever-bright, his smile thinning until it was nothing at all—no charm, no humor, no mask. Just hunger and something darker. The silence between us pressed harder than the ropes cutting into my wrists, every second stretching long and brittle, as if time itself was waiting to see who would break first.

I forced myself still. Every instinct screamed at me to move, to fight, to thrash until something gave. But

I knew if I shifted even an inch, the blade would bite. My pulse didn't care. It thundered against the edge of the knife, begging me to act, daring me to defy him, even though I knew that was exactly what he wanted.

The knife twitched in his grip. Just a fraction, but enough. The steel skimmed higher, grazing the hollow of my throat. My lungs seized. A tremor built in my chest, crawling up my throat, desperate to escape as a sound—a sob, a curse, I didn't know—but I crushed it down until my jaw ached. I would not give him that.

His hand lingered, the pressure feather-light but sharp enough to remind me that it could all be over in a heartbeat. His stare didn't waver. Something flickered behind it—hesitation, memory, calculation, I couldn't tell.

Then, slowly, agonizingly, he eased the knife back. Not far, not enough for me to breathe easier. Just enough for the blade to hover in the narrow space between us, like a promise he hadn't decided whether to keep.

Air rushed into my lungs in a ragged gulp, but relief didn't follow. My chest still felt too tight, my ribs like they were closing in around my heart. Jaxon's grip only tightened on the handle, the tendons in his wrist shifting as though the knife belonged to him more than his own hand.

He wasn't sparing me. He was savoring it.

Jaxon stepped back half a pace, not enough to give me distance, just enough for him to look at me differently. His head tilted, slow and deliberate, like I was something rare and strange he'd stumbled across—something he couldn't decide whether to worship or destroy. His smile didn't return. What replaced it was worse. Curiosity. Calculation.

The knife dangled loose at his side, but angled just enough to lift in an instant. He rolled his shoulder once, casual, as though none of this cost him anything at all.

The space between us wasn't for safety. It was a pause. A cruel one. A held breath in a room that had already stolen too many of mine.

The bulb overhead buzzed and sputtered again, throwing his shadow long across the concrete wall. It jittered with every small movement, larger than life, monstrous in its distortion. The shadow was the Jaxon I remembered from years ago—always too big, always filling the room until there was no space left to breathe.

My wrists burned as the rope dug deeper, my fingers numb where circulation had cut off. I flexed them anyway, feeling the bite of the fibers as a reminder I was still here, still fighting, even if it was just in the smallest ways.

His gaze dipped, following the motion of the ropes, and then slid back up to my face. His lips parted, a breath catching like he might speak. But he didn't. He just watched.

The silence stretched until it didn't feel like silence at all—it felt like pressure. Like the whole room was pressing in, waiting for something to snap. The ropes cut deeper into my wrists with every tremor I fought back, every useless tug of resistance, until I couldn't tell if the wetness I felt was sweat or blood.

Jaxon's eyes dragged over me like he was committing me to memory. Not the way Cassian's gaze did—warmth hidden in sharp edges, a fire that lifted me. Jaxon's was different. He wasn't memorizing me to keep me safe. He was memorizing me to *own* me.

His lips parted, but the sound that came out wasn't a laugh, wasn't even words at first—it was a shaky exhale, heavy with want. He leaned closer, the knife dipping just slightly as if even he forgot it was still in his hand. His other hand rose, fingers brushing the strands of hair stuck to my cheek with a careful tenderness that made my stomach twist. That same hand that had broken bones, split lips, bruised skin—now he was touching me like I was porcelain.

"You were always meant to burn bright," he whispered, his voice hoarse and thick with something that almost sounded like awe. His thumb grazed my jaw, trailing slow, reverent. "But everything bright fades."

The knife hovered, his fingers tracing down my throat like he was both the executioner and the worshipper. My chest heaved, but I forced myself to stay still. If I pulled back, he'd take it as rejection. If I leaned in, he'd take it as surrender.

Then his mouth crashed against mine.

It wasn't a kiss. It was a theft. A demand. His lips were hot, insistent, bruising, and bile rose in my throat so fast I almost gagged. I tried to turn, tried to wrench away, but the ropes held and his grip clamped hard against my jaw.

Revulsion jolted through me. I shoved my head back with every ounce of strength I had left, breath tearing free in a raw rasp. "Don't." My voice cracked, but I forced venom into it anyway. "You don't get to touch me. You don't get to *pretend* this is love."

The change in his face was instant and terrifying.

The reverence shattered. His hand snapped across my face, the crack of skin against skin echoing off the concrete walls like a gunshot. My head whipped sideways, the ropes jerking with the force, fibers tearing into my skin. The copper taste of blood burst across my tongue where my teeth caught my lip.

For a moment, the room swam. My vision blurred with white sparks, tears stinging unbidden, but I blinked hard until the lines steadied. When I turned my face back to him, my cheek stung, my lip throbbed, but I made sure he saw the fire in my eyes.

I would *not* break for him.

Jaxon froze, chest heaving. His knuckles were white around the knife, but his expression wasn't triumph. It was something more unstable. My defiance unsettled him. The fact that I could take his blow, swallow the pain, and still glare back—it rattled him in ways he didn't want to admit.

"You still don't see it," he muttered, voice fraying. He paced half a step, shoulders tense, eyes darting over me like he was both furious and desperate. "I'm not the villain here, Kennedy."

I flexed my wrists against the rope, biting down against the sting as fibers scraped raw skin. My fingers tingled faintly—numbness threatening, but also a reminder that I still had fight left. Somewhere. Somehow.

Jaxon's eyes caught the motion. His gaze snapped back to mine, sharp as a strike, and for a moment neither of us took a breath. He looked at me like he knew exactly what I was doing, and for one horrifying second, I thought he might smile.

But he didn't.

He just stared at me, knife trembling faintly in his grip, chest rising and falling too fast, too uneven. He looked like a man standing at the edge of something—worship or destruction, I couldn't tell which—and I was the only thing holding him there.

My wrists burned as I flexed again, the ropes biting deeper, fibers peeling at skin already raw. Pain flared up my arms, sharp and electric, but I clung to it. Pain meant I could still feel. Pain meant I was still here.

Cassian's voice pulsed at the back of my skull like a heartbeat. Don't hesitate. It had felt like overprotectiveness in his apartment; now it felt like prophecy. The words weren't a warning anymore—they were a map.I shifted, slow, careful, testing the slack at the edges of the knots. Every tiny movement scraped fire across my skin. The rope gave nothing back. But I wasn't looking for freedom yet. I was looking for reach. For the cool press of metal I'd prayed had survived the struggle, still hidden, still waiting.

The pocketknife. My back pocket.

Jaxon's gaze dipped to my hands, then back to my face. I froze, breath locked in my chest. His eyes narrowed—not suspicion, not yet. Just scrutiny. A tilt of his head, like he couldn't decide if I was crumbling or planning.

I let my shoulders sag. Dropped my chin so my hair fell forward, a red curtain between me and the hunger in his eyes. My wrists twitched behind me, subtle as a pulse.

He stepped closer, boots dragging echoes across the concrete. The air thickened with each movement, shrinking the space I had left to breathe. His fingers caught my chin again, tilting my head up until I was forced to meet his stare.

"You're shaking," he murmured. Softer now. Almost tender. His thumb brushed the corner of my lip, collecting the trace of blood there. He stared at it for a moment too long, then dragged his thumb slowly across his tongue. His eyes fluttered shut like he was savoring it.

Revulsion rose hard in my throat, but I forced it down. Not yet. I flexed my wrists again, fingers reaching, inching back, nails scraping at rough fabric, at skin, at nothing. My heart pounded so loud it felt like he could hear it—like he could follow the sound straight to the secret I clung to.

The knife was there. It had to be.

I reached again, a hair deeper this time, and my nail caught the cold, unmistakable kiss of metal against the side of my finger. A surge of relief threatened to break my mask, but I crushed it down, keeping my face slack and blank.

Jaxon's head flicked to the side at some faint noise—a drip, a rustle, something behind the door. He straightened slowly, knife still in hand, scanning the shadows. Then, as if deciding it wasn't worth his attention, he let out a soft chuckle, sheathed the blade at his hip, and reached for something heavier on a nearby crate.

A gun. Matte black. He turned it once in his palm like it was nothing more than a toy.

My heart slammed hard enough to hurt.

He dragged a chair from the corner with a screech that echoed off the concrete and set it down directly in front of me. Calm. Methodical. He sat, legs spread, elbows on his knees, the gun loose in one hand, the other resting on his thigh. Like we were just two people having a quiet talk.

Except he was holding all the power.

"You know..." he began, voice soft, almost conversational. "I used to picture this differently. You crying. Begging. Maybe even trying to talk me down. But you're not, are you? You're just sitting there, pretending you're still in control."

The sound of the gun tapping against his knee echoed sharp in the concrete room, each hollow knock ratcheting the tension tighter. My skin crawled.

"That's what I always loved about you," he said. "That fire. That delusion. That's what makes this all the more fun."

The words slithered under my skin, sharp and cloying all at once. My wrists twitched again, the blade inched deeper into the rope, sawing silently, each strand straining.

He leaned in, slow and deliberate, his free hand lifting until his thumb brushed across my cheekbone. The touch was soft, almost reverent, but it curdled in my skin like poison. Revulsion clawed up my throat before I could stop it.

Disgust surged before I could stop it. I snapped my head to the side and spat, sharp and fast. The sound cracked through the silence like a slap.

For a beat, Jaxon froze, spit glistening against his cheek. His eyes widened—not at the insult itself, but at the audacity. Then he laughed. Low, humorless, a sound grated raw with irritation. The kind of laugh that said I'd just made things worse for myself. He swiped the back of his hand across his face, smearing it away, his grin twisting sharp and dangerous.

Cassian's face flashed in my head—his hand on my chin, his voice low against my mouth. *You come back to me, Wildfire.* My throat locked.

Jaxon saw it. His smile sharpened.

"Delusional." Disgust escaped his lips. "Do you want to know why he was really there that night? Why he kept showing up like a bad habit?"

The rope gave a little more, fibers snapping like faint fireworks in the silence. I clenched my jaw, but he didn't wait for an answer.

"Your father paid him," Jaxon said softly. "Paid him to make you disappear in the most finite of ways."

The words landed like a drop of acid, eating their way down into bone.

"You're lying," I whispered, forcing my voice steady even as my stomach churned.

The words didn't make sense. My dad? No. That wasn't—he wouldn't—

He laughed, low and hollow. "Am I? You really believed it, didn't you?" His voice went almost tender. "That he was different? But you were just a job."

My pulse hammered. The rope gave another inch, and I nearly gasped with it.

He straightened in his chair, the gun dangling casually from his fingers. "You should thank me," he murmured. "At least I'm telling you the truth before the end. He won't."

The last strand of rope split beneath my blade. My wrists were free.

Something in me snapped.

I lunged, the knife flashing free from behind my back as I surged up from the chair. The rope that had held me clattered to the floor. Jaxon's eyes widened, but only for a heartbeat—then his arm came up, blocking, deflecting. The blade skittered across his forearm instead of sinking into his chest, a thin line of red blossoming against his skin.

He snarled and drove his shoulder into me, slamming me back against the chair so hard the legs screeched across the concrete. The air punched out of my lungs, the knife nearly slipping from my hand. I slashed wild, forcing him a step back, but he was already recovering, already pressing in again.

I swung again—desperate, clumsy—but he caught my wrist this time, wrenching it up until my knuckles popped. The knife clattered from my fingers, skidding across the floor into shadow.

Panic spiked sharp, but I didn't freeze. My free elbow snapped back, driving into his ribs with everything I had. The sound it dragged out of him was ugly and wet, more bark than gasp, but his grip faltered. I shoved forward, twisting, trying to rip free.

He came back fast, angrier, his other hand clamping around my throat, shoving me back into the wall. My head cracked against the concrete, sparks bursting across my vision. Black spots danced at the edges.

The gun was still in his right hand. Still raised.

I saw my only chance. My body moved before my mind could catch up. I slammed my elbow again, this time catching his wrist and smashing it against the wall. Once. Twice. The impact jolted up my arm, rattling my bones, but I didn't stop.

On the third hit, his hand spasmed. The gun clattered to the ground between us.

Both of us dove.

My fingers scraped cold metal a split second before his. He roared, lunging, but I twisted, rolling onto my back, and brought the weapon up between us. His weight crushed down, his hands clawing for mine, but I jammed the barrel under his jaw, right against the frantic pulse in his throat.

"Don't fucking move," I rasped, my voice raw, shaking.

For the first time all night, Jaxon froze. His breath was hot against my face, eyes wide, wild, the fight still there but leashed by the cold steel digging into his skin.

My hands trembled around the grip, but I didn't lower it. Not an inch.

The gun dug into his throat, but he was heavier, stronger. His hand shot out, shoving against my wrist, the other clawing at my shoulder until my back slammed against the concrete. The impact rattled my bones, the air tearing from my lungs. The gun slipped sideways, my grip faltering as his weight crushed me down.

He snarled, trying to rip it free. I clung with both hands, the cold metal biting into my palms as we wrestled for control, the weapon twisting between us. His knee drove into my ribs, pain exploding white-hot until stars burst behind my eyes.

The gun jerked sideways under his grip—my finger caught the trigger.

The blast tore through the bunker like a thunderclap, deafening, a flash of recoil slamming back into my chest. For a heartbeat, I didn't understand. My ears rang, my arms shook.

Then Jaxon's body jerked hard against mine, his eyes going wide. Blood bloomed across his shirt, hot and wet between us. His grip slipped, the fight stuttering out of him as he sagged against me.

I shoved upward, twisting out from under him. He hit the floor on his knees, then crumpled to his side, one hand pressed to the spreading stain. His breath came ragged, wet.

"The man you love," he rasped, voice shredded and low. "He was meant to end you."

The words slithered out like poison. His eyes flicked up, finding mine, something almost like triumph flickering through the pain. His lips parted as if to say more, but the sound never came.

I staggered back, the weapon still in my grip, my arms trembling. My chest heaved, breath sawing raw through my throat. The metallic taste of blood mixed with gunpowder burned on my tongue.

The gun was still in my hands. My arms shook with the weight of it, too heavy, too cold, like the steel had fused to my bones. My breath tore ragged, the bunker spinning around me, shadows leering in and out with every flicker of the bulb.

Jaxon lay twisted on the concrete, his eyes glassy but still open, his blood crawling outward in dark rivers that reached for my boots. The smell hit me then—copper and smoke, acrid and choking.

My stomach lurched. I wanted to drop the gun, wanted to scream, wanted to claw the air from my lungs. But I didn't. My fingers wouldn't open. They clenched tighter, as if letting go would undo what had already been done.

His voice lingered, echoing in my skull even though he was gone. *He was meant to end you..*

The sound of it was louder than the gunshot. Louder than the pounding in my head.

The door slammed open.

I spun before thought could catch up. My arms jerked the gun up, sights leveled, finger trembling on the trigger.

And there—framed in the doorway, chest heaving, eyes wild and locked on me—was Cassian.

He froze when he saw me. His gaze cut once to Jaxon's body sprawled on the ground, then to the gun shaking in my hands, then back to my face.

"Ken—" His voice broke on the word. He lifted his hands, palms open, like he was staring down a wild animal. Like I might bolt—or bite.

My grip tightened. My chest heaved. "Stay back."

The words scraped raw, but they came out steady enough. He'd told me once not to hesitate, and I didn't. Not now. Not when every nerve screamed that trust had just become a loaded weapon.

"Is it true?" I whispered, but the barrel didn't lower.

Kennedy

19

Is it true?

The question ripped out of me like shrapnel. I hadn't planned to say it—not like that, not so bare—but once it was out, hanging sharp and ugly in the space between us, I couldn't drag it back. I couldn't pretend I didn't already know the answer.

Cassian didn't flinch.

He didn't rush to deny it. Didn't stammer or explode or play dumb. He didn't even look *guilty*. No wide eyes. No stumbling over excuses.

He simply stilled.

A slow, terrible stillness. The kind of stillness that came from a man who'd been waiting for this moment.

Bracing for it. Knowing, on some level, that one day I would turn on him with a weapon in my hands.

And I had.

The gun shook in my grip, but I kept it level. My arms screamed with effort. My ribs ached beneath every breath, raw from impact. My heartbeat hammered against my sternum like it was trying to break free of my chest altogether. Sweat stung the raw split in my lip, catching on the copper taste of blood. My whole body trembled so hard I could hear the faint tap of the gun clicking against my own pulse.

He didn't move.

Didn't even *blink.*

He looked at me the way he always did—direct, unwavering, as if he refused to treat me like something fragile. Even standing in front of him with a loaded gun between us—he still saw me as an equal *threat.* Equal power. Equal fire.

I didn't know whether to hate him for it or shatter at the sight of it.

"Are you just going to stand there?" I whispered. My voice barely made it past my throat. "Answer me."

Cassian's jaw flexed. His hands stayed down at his sides, open, visible. No sudden moves. No reaching for his own gun. He was being calculated—but not cruelly. Not manipulatively. Carefully. Like he was trying to give me room to decide.

To choose.

"Kennedy," he said at last.

My name. Nothing else.

And that—more than any confession—was what nearly broke me.

A low growl hummed in my throat. "Answer me."

He exhaled once, slow and deliberate, like he was steadying himself before stepping into fire. His throat worked, his fists clenching just barely before relaxing once more. He could've lied. He could've said no. He could've said anything to make me lower the gun.

But instead—

"It wasn't supposed to be you," he said quietly.

The words hit like the floor tilting beneath me. The ground shifting. The room spinning with them.

"Wh—"

"Not now," he cut in gently, voice still low, controlled. "Lets get out of here first and I'll tell you everything you want to know."

The reminder of Jaxon's corpse made my stomach twist. I hadn't looked down—not once. If I did, I didn't know which part of me would break first—the guilt, the fear, or the numbness.

Cassian took one step closer.

I jerked the gun higher, right over his heart.

"Don't," I snapped.

He stilled instantly.

Not because he was scared.

But because he was listening.

That — that was Cassian. He heard everything. Even what I didn't say.

His voice softened. Not weak—never weak—but rough at the edges, like gravel dragged over steel. "I get it. You don't trust me, and you shouldn't."

The honesty cut deeper than any denial ever could have.

He took another step. Not lunging. Not charging. Just closing the distance one breath at a time.

"Let's be honest Ken, if you were going to shoot me," he murmured, "you would have done it already. Put the gun down."

My eyes stung. I hated that they did.

"No," I whispered. "You don't get to control this. Me."

He swallowed hard. His expression finally cracked—just a flicker, but it was there. Pain. Regret. Longing. All tangled up in an exhaustion I knew only came from fighting wars no one else could see.

"I just want to get you out of here. Do you really want to stick around?" he said, his eyes flicking between Jaxon's lifeless body and me.

The fight went out of my arms before it ever left my chest. My whole body sagged, but I kept the barrel up even as my wrists shook beneath its weight.

Cassian moved like he knew my breaking point down to the inch. Like he felt the tremors in my muscles before I did. He closed the last few steps slowly, deliberately, until the warmth of his body brushed the front of mine—not touching, but close enough to feel like a gravity I couldn't turn away from.

His breath ghosted against my ear, low and even.

"Give me the gun, Wildfire."

The name splintered something that had been barely holding together.

A tremor ran through me—not out of fear.

But out of grief.

Grief for the version of me that had believed love could be simple. Grief for the version of him who had let me believe it.

My fingers faltered.

Cassian's hand rose—not grabbing, not prying. Just hovering. Waiting for permission.

Slowly, painfully, I let my hand fall into his.

He took the weapon — gently, reverently.

The second he did, I ripped my hand away like his touch had scalded me.

His face didn't change. But something in his eyes flinched.

Not at the pain of me pulling away.

But with the knowledge that this — *us* — could never go back to what it was before.

Cassian didn't reach again. Didn't try. He just stood there—gun now in his hand, blood cooling in a dark pool not three feet away, the metallic scent of it mingling with damp concrete and smoke. The bunker suddenly felt smaller. Too quiet. Too full of everything neither of us was saying.

My throat burned. "What do we do about him?" My voice came out thin, raw. "We can't just leave him here."

Cassian's jaw tightened, his answer clipped. "We can't stay either. Don't worry, I'll make sure he's taken care of when you're safe."

The words sank heavy between us. I didn't look at Jaxon again. Couldn't.

It wasn't forgiveness. It wasn't even pity. Just the truth that once, he'd been a part of me—and now he never would be again.

Because even after everything—after the fear, the lies, the blood—I couldn't shut off the part of me that used to care. That old, stubborn softness refused to die, no matter how many times the world tried to burn it out of me.

I'd loved him once—the boy who laughed too loud, who said forever like it meant something. The memory of love still twisted through the ruin of it.

I hated that it still meant something. I hated that my heart didn't know how to stop loving people who broke it.

Cassian's eyes stayed on me, sharp and searching, but I refused to look at him. If I did—if I met that gaze I knew too well, the one that had once felt like safety—I was afraid I'd break. Or worse, forgive.

"Okay, let's go then," I said, my voice raw but steady. Not a plea. Not permission. A command.

He didn't argue.

But he didn't turn his back on me either.

He shifted like he meant to take the lead—only to stop himself halfway through the motion. His jaw clenched. His grip tightened on the gun. Then he angled his body slightly, gesturing me forward.

I didn't move.

I wouldn't.

Not with his weapon in his hand. Not with the truth hanging between us like a live wire.

His throat worked once, hard. Then he took a step instead, moving past me—slowly, carefully—like I was a cornered animal he didn't want to spook. Another foot forward. Then he stopped just ahead, giving me space to follow.

I didn't.

I mirrored him instead, stepping just far enough to close the gap without falling behind. Refusing to trail him. Refusing to lead.

His gaze flickered to mine at the edge of his vision. Not quite, surprise. Not quite approval. Just... acknowledgement.

Neither of us said a word.

We moved together like that—side by side, shoulder to shoulder, not touching but orbiting, tethered by something neither of us trusted anymore but couldn't break free from. Our footsteps echoed in near-perfect rhythm against concrete, fading into dirt as the bunker's mouth spilled us into damp night air.

The forest was black and breathless around us. Leaves whispered. Somewhere far off, an owl called. The world felt painfully alive compared to what we'd left behind.

Cassian paused at the tree line, waiting without looking back.

I stopped beside him.

We stayed like that for a moment—two statues carved from adrenaline and betrayal, breathing in the same night, refusing to give ground.

Then he spoke—quiet, low, controlled. "The car's this way."

He angled his body slightly, inviting me to walk ahead.

I didn't.

"I'm not turning my back on you," I said.

He didn't sigh. Didn't argue. He simply nodded once, as if that was fair.

We walked.

Side by side.

The door groaned behind us as we slipped out into the night, shutting Jaxon's body back into the dark like a secret neither of us were ready to accept. The air outside hit cold and wet against my skin, thick with moss and damp soil and iron—like the world itself still smelled of blood. The wind crept beneath my clothes, threading through my hair, lifting the sweat-stuck strands at my temples. My whole body trembled, not entirely from cold.

Cassian stayed a step to my right, his presence shadowing mine without touching. Even now, when I could still feel the ghost of his breath against my ear from where he'd whispered Give me the gun, he kept distance like he knew I'd set myself on fire before I let him lay a hand on me.

The trees swallowed us whole as we stepped off the crumbling concrete slab and back onto the dirt path. Branches arched overhead like spines, jagged and clawed, blotting out whatever meager light the sky might've offered. Every step sank into damp leaves and soft mud. The forest floor swallowed our footsteps like it was complicit.

Neither of us spoke. Words would've felt too loud. Too clumsy. Too human.

Silence wasn't quiet. Silence was its own language.

At one point, my foot caught a stray root. Instinct made me reach out, to steady myself — and instinct made his hand twitch like he meant to catch me. We both froze before contact could happen.

We continued to move forward, because stopping would've meant thinking.

The trees began to loosen around us, branches thinning until the night opened wider above our heads. Gravel replaced dirt beneath my boots, the crunch of it too loud in the quiet.

The car sat where the trees broke, quiet and still, like it had been holding its breath for us.

Sienna was in the driver's seat.

Not slumped. Not trembling. Just… upright.

Too upright. Too composed. Like she'd braced herself so hard she'd forgotten how to move.

I knew that posture. I lived it — back straight, breath locked, mistaking stillness for strength because anything else would've meant shattering.

But there was no strength in her stillness.

Only shock.

Only silence pressed into bone.

"Wait," Cassian breathed, more to the shadows than to me, and I felt the air in him change. That coiled stillness snapped tighter, like wire pulled taut. "Stay behind me."

I should've listened. I didn't. Stubbornness dragged me sideways. I didn't want him between me and the life I was still trying to reach. The lot was a slab of black glass. The car's windows were a darker slice inside the dark, reflecting nothing. I rounded the bumper, hand landing on the back handle before I could think.

The door lifted on a breath of cold air and old coffee. And then hands—two—shot forward from the dark and yanked.

I didn't even have the breath to scream. One arm hooked under mine, the other across my collarbone. My back slammed into someone's chest. A forearm locked around my throat—not choking, *containing.* Pure restraint. Efficient. Like I weighed nothing.

I *did not* go quietly.

I twisted, slammed my elbow back hard. It connected with ribs. The grip around me flexed—not in pain, but in irritation.

"Easy, sweetheart," the man behind me murmured, voice bored like he was wrangling a drunk at closing time. "You should tell your girl to calm down," he added over my shoulder. "She's only making it worse for herself."

Don't hurt her!" Sienna's voice cracked like glass from the driver's seat. She was rigid behind the wheel, hands welded at ten and two, mascara streaked like war paint down her face.

A boot thudded on the floorboard. A muzzle pressed hard against her temple. The man beside me hissed, low and venomous: "Shut. Up." Each word a warning, not a suggestion.

Sienna flinched like the barrel was fire. Her breath caught — held — like she was afraid even exhaling too loud would get her shot.

A second man leaned forward out of the backseat gloom on my other side, his bicep boxing me in. I felt the brush of his coat, the click of a safety flicked off like a tongue tsking.

I couldn't see Cassian, but I felt him—the way the air shifted in front of the open door, the click-whisper of leather and steel as he drew and sighted without a wasted thought.

"Let her go," he said, calm enough to make my heart lurch. "We can talk."

"Drop it," the man at my throat said, voice still mild. "Or I open her from ear to ear."

For a breath I thought Cassian would test the math anyway—he was fast enough, I'd seen it. Then I remembered the look in his eyes when I pointed a gun at him: not fear, not pride. Calculation chained to love. His muzzle dipped. He set the gun on the gravel with a deliberate clink, boot nudging it under the car.

"Hands," the man on my left said. Cassian lifted them, empty and slow, palms forward.

"Get in," the stranger demanded.

Cassian didn't move at first. He just stood there, spine straight, jaw clenched — the kind of stillness that wasn't compliance but choice.

Then he walked. Slow. Unrushed. Every step measured like he was counting the beats until he'd take theirs. He opened the passenger door himself and got in.

"Drive," the one behind me told Sienna, that same pleasant tone that felt like a hand on the back of your head before it went under water. "Back to the road. Right at the fork. You know where."

Sienna nodded once, a shaking bird of a motion, and the car rolled like it was leaving the earth begrudgingly. Cassian moved when they told him—front passenger seat, slow, controlled, tension making architecture of his shoulders. He didn't look at me. He didn't need to. I felt his attention like heat. My pulse settled into a drumbeat I knew too well: not calm, not panic. Readiness. I hated him a little for gifting me that.

We hit asphalt. Trees thinned into the suggestion of houses, then none at all. The night breathed different out here, bigger, emptier. The men didn't talk. The one holding me adjusted his grip once, not cruel, just practiced. The other watched Cassian with an interest that wasn't curiosity. Sizing him, the way predators admire other predators.

Cassian's voice came soft, slanting back without turning his head. "Ken."

My name in his mouth felt like something I wasn't ready to hold. "Don't," I said, and it bled out like a plea.

He didn't push. He let the word settle and fade.

Outside, a signpost flashed by—just a rectangle of reflective nothing, but familiar in a way that made my stomach drop. The road narrowed, then curved, climbing. Memory rose like smoke: childhood drives where windows were always rolled up, where you were told this wasn't the kind of place you mentioned to anyone. The kind of place called a "retreat" with a smile that never reached a single eye.

Sienna's knuckles were bone white where they clutched the wheel. Sweat slicked the steering wheel leather. Every breath she took sounded like it might shake her to pieces.

"Straight," the man behind me murmured. "Then left at the gate."

And then the gate came into view — black iron with that same pretentious crest welded into the center. My father's. Of course. I didn't need to look twice. I knew every line of it. Every curl of metal. Every inch of it whispered, *You weren't taken somewhere new. You were brought back.*

My throat closed. "No," I whispered, without meaning to. The word fogged the glass and vanished. "No."

A keypad blinked on a stone pillar. The man leaned forward and rattled off numbers. Sienna's shaking hand hovered over the keys, then punched them in. The light turned green with an obedient little chime. The iron slid aside.

The drive up was long and smug and perfectly lit—ground lights throwing up tasteful little cones like my terror should be grateful for the ambiance. Gravel whispered under the tires. Trees peeled back to reveal the house itself, all permission and power: stucco and glass and stone, low and wide, designed to look like it had grown there on purpose. It hadn't. It had been planted, aggressively.

A small ocean of lawn unfurled to the right. To the left, a motor court where cars slept like well-fed beasts.

Cassian's profile was carved out of night, jaw a hard line, eyes forward and blazing. He knew the place. Whether he'd been the shadow invited here or the shadow avoided, I didn't know. Didn't want to.

The car rolled to a stop. The engine ticked once. Twice.

"Out," the man at my throat said, cheerful as a host ushering guests to cocktails. His arm unhooked from me only to use me like a handle, propelling me across the seat. The other man eased his barrel off Cassian's ribs and gave him a nod that was almost respectful.

Sienna stumbled out on shaking legs, catching herself against the door frame like the car had tried to buck her off.

The front door didn't open — it was *forced*. One of the men shoved it wide with his boot like he owned the place. Light didn't spill out so much as *glared*, bright and artificial, bleaching the night off our skin.

A butler-looking man in a suit stood there, stiff and silent, hands clasped like he wished he was anywhere else. He didn't greet us. Didn't ask questions. He just stepped aside — not for us, but for the *display* we were about to become.

They herded us inside without ceremony. Sienna stumbled over the threshold, catching herself on polished marble before one of them grabbed her by the back of her collar and shoved her forward again. I followed because I was dragged. Cassian only moved when one of the barrels nudged him between the shoulders — slow, deliberate, like he was making them work for every inch.

A set of double doors waited at the end of the hall. One of the men kicked them open.

Michael's office. Mahogany. Leather. Glass. A room designed to intimidate before a word was spoken.

Sienna was shoved forward first. She tripped over the rug and hit the floor hard. I was yanked after her — knees catching polished wood, palms slapping down to break the fall.

Cassian didn't fall. They tried to make him.

One of the men grabbed his shoulder and drove him toward the ground. Cassian moved like a reflex — not wild, not reckless. Precise. Deadly. His elbow cracked against a man's jaw. Another fist followed. A second man went stumbling into a bookshelf. A third barely got his hands up in time.

Chairs toppled. Glass shattered. Someone swore blood out of their teeth.

"Get him down!" one barked, voice strained.

It took three of them to hold him — and even pinned, he strained like a loaded wire, muscles coiled as if he could snap all of them with one good breath.

And then—A voice cut through the room. Smooth. Unhurried. Bored.

"Are we done throwing a tantrum?"

The air shifted. Not with fear — with humiliation.

Heads snapped toward the doorway. Cassian stilled, chest heaving, but refused to kneel. The guards held him but didn't dare tighten their grip.

Michael Royal stepped into view like he'd been standing there the whole time, waiting for the perfect moment to make his disappointment known. His suit was immaculate. His expression flat. Not a hair out of place.

He looked at the chaos — the overturned chair, the blood on the floor — and his lip barely twitched.

"Alright that's enough, let him go. If he's going to make a scene, he can at least do it with some dignity."

"Sweetheart," he said, and every syllable was a smothering hand. "You've had quite the adventure tonight, haven't you?"

My skin tried to crawl off my bones.

Cassian didn't speak. Didn't move. But the air around him changed—denser, darker, threaded tight with a fury he held the way other men held a weapon. The men at my sides eased back half a step, like even they understood they'd ushered a match and a fuse into the same room.

"Michael! Let her go, damn it!" Cassian said, voice quiet as a clipped wire.

Michael's smile did something delicate and ugly. "She's home," he said, as if he were granting me something. "I'll take care of her from here."

My laugh was a small, sharp thing that surprised even me. "Yeah, like you always have. Right dad?"

He held the perfect smile, the perfect calm — but I knew better. He was thinking. Scrambling. Deciding whether to silence me or let me dig my own grave.

I took another step. The night air was sharp against my skin, slipping through every split and bruise like it belonged there. I could taste the bitterness rising in my mouth — all the years of swallowing what wasn't true, all the ways love had been used against me.

Jaxon's last words scraped the inside of my skull: *The man you love, he was meant to end you.*

The men's hands hovered—close enough to remind me they existed, not close enough to matter if I decided to set myself on fire.

Behind me, Cassian shifted a fraction, enough to cast his shadow over my shoulder without touching me. "Kennedy," he said, just my name, steady as a hand on a spine.

"Save the theatrics," Michael said lightly. "Stand her up. I'd rather have this conversation face to face."

He didn't wait to see if they obeyed. He turned his back on all of us — on the guns, the blood, the struggle — and crossed to the liquor cart like he was selecting a soundtrack. Crystal clinked against crystal as he poured amber into two heavy glasses, the sound obscenely domestic in the tension. He didn't offer one. He simply held both — weighing which of us deserved acknowledgement.

"What—over drinks?" My voice shook. My hands didn't. "Before or after you explain how many people you paid to erase me?"

Something alive flashed behind his eyes and was gone. "You're upset," he said gently.

"You're stalling," Cassian said, and every consonant carried a promise.

The wind lifted, cold and clean, and in that sliver of air the truth stood up between us like a third person.

The house loomed, patient. The men adjusted their grips. Sienna's breath hitched into something that could turn into a sob if she let it.

Michael's smile returned, bright and bloodless. "Leave." He refused to look away from me. "You two idiots — out. And take the other girl with you."

The hands that seized Sienna this time were brutal. She stumbled as they yanked her backward, heels scraping against the floor.

"Wait—wait, *don't*—" Her voice cracked, reaching for me even when her body couldn't. "Kennedy!"

I lurched up on instinct, but a forearm slammed across my chest, forcing me back. Wood bit into my spine. Sienna's fingers clawed at the air like she could catch mine if she just reached hard enough.

"Where are you taking her?" My voice tore out of me, raw and useless.

One of the men barked something I didn't catch. My cry hit the wall of their indifference and vanished. Sienna's sob fractured into a choke as they dragged her past the threshold, her eyes wide and wild, locked on mine until the door swallowed her whole.

Silence followed—not empty.

Heavy.

Michael let it settle like dust after an explosion. He set his untouched glass down on the desk, the crystal clicking softly against the wood.

Then he looked at me—only me.

"Now," he said calmly. "Where were we?"

Kennedy

20

S ilence stopped feeling like silence.

It swelled. Thickened. Pressed against my eardrums until I could hear my own pulse in it — frantic and animal. It wasn't quiet. It was restraint.

Michael stood across the room with the kind of stillness men wore when violence was their second language. He didn't sit. He didn't pace. He waited, like a judge deciding whether to bother with the sentencing or skip straight to the execution.

"Do you know what I hate most?" he asked softly. "Ingratitude."

The words weren't loud, but they carried like smoke. He lifted his glass and rolled the amber liquid once — slow

— watching me over the rim like he was deciding which part of me to burn first.

"I give, and give, and give — protection, resources, opportunities — and still, somehow, I'm cast as the villain."

His tone didn't rise. It didn't need to. Rage wasn't loud in him. It was controlled. Sterile. Surgical.

His gaze slid to Cassian. Brief. Cutting. Like a man glancing at a defect in a weapon he'd paid too much for.

"But then," he said lightly, "some people really do earn the title."

He set the glass down without drinking. The crystal kissed the wood with a sound too gentle for the threat hanging beneath it.

"Let's start with your mother."

The words landed like a slap I hadn't braced for.

I didn't move. Didn't breathe. I wasn't sure I could. Her name hadn't been spoken in that house in years — not because she was dead, but because Michael acted as if she never existed.

Now he said *mother* like it was an inconvenience. An obstacle. A mess he'd been forced to clean.

"She was clever," he went on, not bothering to disguise the irritation beneath the praise. "Terminal illness makes some women bold, I suppose. With nothing left to lose, she got… creative."

His hand drifted along the edge of the desk as he spoke, fingers brushing the polished wood like he was narrating a presentation rather than unearthing a grave.

"She started collecting things. Bank transfers. Shell accounts. Offshore deposits. Names. Even bodies, when she could trace them." His mouth twitched — not regret. Nostalgia. "Years of work. Years of loyalty. All wrapped up and hand-delivered to some third-rate attorney downtown."

I could feel Cassian beside me — motionless but strung so tight he could've snapped steel.

Michael didn't look at either of us.

"She gave him instructions. The day you turned twenty-five, he walks into my office and presents me with an ultimatum. Either I hand over half of everything I own, half of my money… or he hands my dirty deeds to the police."

A buzzing started in my ears. Static. Rage. Grief. I didn't know.

My hands curled into fists before I realized they'd moved.

Michael's eyes finally flicked back to mine.

"So I did what any man in my position would do." He said it like it was obvious. Inevitable. "I hired someone to remove the problem."

The room tilted. Not visibly. Not physically. But something in the air shifted like the center of gravity had moved.

He didn't make me ask.

"And that," he said, gesturing lazily toward Cassian without turning his head, "is where he came in."

Blood roared in my ears.

"He knew your name. He knew your face. To him, you were an assignment. A transaction. A location on a map."

The next words weren't loud.

They didn't have to be.

"I handed her to you on a silver platter — and you couldn't even do your fucking job."

Michael didn't raise his voice but directed towards Cassian.

He smiled. Like he was reciting a joke only he understood.

"You disappoint me, Cassian," he said softly — almost like a father scolding a child for breaking a vase. "One target. One clean solution. And instead…"

His gaze cut between the two of us — sharp as a scalpel beneath the charm.

"You got attached."

He scoffed. "You. The man with eighty-seven confirmed kills. And *she* was the line you wouldn't cross?"

Silence swallowed the room.

Not shock. Not denial. Recognition.

Cassian didn't move. Didn't argue. He stood and took it like a man already condemned — like he'd rehearsed this reckoning in his head long before it ever reached his ears.

My body refused to decide what to feel. Fury. Betrayal. Relief. Revulsion. They all punched through me at once until I couldn't tell if I was breathing or choking.

Attached.

Like that was all I was. Some complication. A mission gone sideways because a trained killer tripped over feelings.

I wanted to scream at Cassian. I wanted to defend him. I wanted to claw out of my own skin.

Before I could decide who to be — judge, executioner, or coward — Cassian finally moved.

Not much. Just a shift of breath. A slow turn of his head. But it felt like the whole damn room rotated with him.

When his eyes found mine, it wasn't pleading.

It was surrender. Not the weak kind. The kind soldiers gave when they laid down arms not because they were beaten — but because they refused to spill blood that didn't deserve it.

"Kennedy."

My name, steady and grounded — like he was forcing me to stay here. To hear him.

"I took the job," he said. "They handed me a file with everything I needed to know about you."

He didn't blink.

"They put your life in a file and I treated it like any typical target—and then I saw you."

The air tightened. My throat with it.

"You looked at me like I was human." His hands flexed once at his sides, restrained fists aching to be used. "It was as if I forgot you were my mission."

He wasn't asking for forgiveness.

He was handing me the knife.

"I should've walked away right then. Reported failure. Cut ties and taken whatever consequence came with it." His jaw clenched. "But I didn't."

His voice dropped — not softer, but closer. Like he was no longer speaking across the room, but straight into my bones.

"I stayed. Not because of guilt. Not because I grew a conscience overnight."

He paused.

"I stayed because for the first time in years… I wanted something that wasn't written in blood."

Silence stretched — thick and trembling, like a glass about to shatter.

"I won't insult you by asking for trust," he finished quietly. "But don't let him," his gaze flicked to Michael like a blade, "reduce what happened between us to a miscalculation."

Cassian didn't move after he spoke. Didn't so much as sway. But somehow, everything else did — or maybe it was just me. My balance tilted. My heartbeat scraped against my ribs in uneven bursts. I wasn't looking at a man. I was looking at a verdict being willingly delivered.

Michael watched him with eerie stillness.

Not like a man betrayed.

Like a man inconvenienced.

He studied Cassian the way one might study a hairline crack in a priceless vase — mildly irritated that it existed, already deciding how best to replace it.

Then he gave the smallest, most unimpressed exhale. Barely a breath. A puff of air through his nose.

"That's very touching," Michael said, as if reviewing a Hallmark card. "Truly. If I had a heart, I'm sure it would've stirred."

He took two unhurried steps back toward his desk, movements measured like music without melody. He didn't sit. He didn't look away. He lifted his glass, not to drink — but to pause.

"So let's make something clear," he murmured, voice dipped in silk so fine it cut. "This isn't a love story. No."

The words fell like a switch being flipped.

Something shifted behind him — not metaphorical. Literal.

The faint slide of a drawer broke the silence, sharp as a fault line. Wood scraped, a soft metallic chime following — the unmistakable weight of something being lifted.

I didn't have to look to know what it was.

When I finally did, the gun was already in Michael's hand — steady, sure, inevitable.

No rush.

No flourish.

Just inevitability.

Cassian reacted — not visibly, not dramatically. But I felt it beside me, like a storm tightening its muscles before breaking. His weight shifted forward. Shoulders squared. A breath hitched sharp through his chest — the kind you hear right before violence erupts.

Michael didn't even glance at him.

The barrel of the gun rose — and leveled with my head.

Not between the eyes. Slightly above.

Calculated. Prepared. Already imagined.

"Don't."

The word was quiet enough to make everything else in the room feel too loud. The air conditioner. My pulse. My own breath clawing its way out of my throat.

"You've already proven you don't follow orders," Michael said, as lightly as if we were discussing spilled wine. "Don't make me clean up your mess twice."

His wrist flicked once.

"To your knees."

He didn't wait for me to decide.

The butt of the pistol cracked across my temple with a sound that split the air and an ache that seared white into my skull. Pain flashed, hot and immediate; something warm ran down my cheek and I tasted metal. My knees hit the floor before thought could bargain with muscle. I stayed there, stunned, palm pressed to the hardwood to hold myself steady while the world swam.

"Stay on your knees!" Michael commanded, the gun an extension of the command.

From the doorway a voice answered — calm, clear, professional. "Mr. Royal, put the gun down. Keep your hands where we can see them."

Michael moved like a man taking inventory. His hand closed in my hair and he hauled me up so fast my feet skimmed the floor. He planted me in front of him, body rigid, and wrapped his arm across my chest; the barrel kissed the side of my head, cold and absolute. He didn't cradle me. He used me. My face was forced to the side, and I could feel his breath, hot and controlled, in the hollow behind my ear.

The sound of other boots filled in behind that voice: measured, tactical, the quiet roar of people who had practiced patience until it was a weapon. The geometry of the room changed; positions were taken, angles considered. Michael's little empire thinned at the edges.

He turned his head only enough to sneer at the doorway, the gun never leaving my temple. Annoyance curled his mouth. "You're trespassing," he said, as if that fact could buy him time.

"It's a crime scene now," the officer said. "Drop the weapon and step away slowly."

Michael's knuckles whitened where they gripped my ribs. He leaned in so close I could hear the tick of his pulse.

"One move," he warned softly, eyes cutting toward the officers crowding the doorway, "and she dies."

Cassian moved closer, slow and deliberate, until he was just a breath away. He didn't lunge. Didn't shout. He made himself a presence — a wall between Michael's aim and the doorway, close enough that I could feel the heat of him at my back even with Michael's grip still locked around me. His fingers flexed once, slow and private, the only sign of restraint left in him.

And then, in the smallest opening — the fraction of a second when Michael's attention flicked from the officer to the tactical spread in the hall — Cassian uncoiled.

Cassian didn't reach for the gun.

He reached for him.

His arm swept under Michael's, ripping his hold off my chest with so much force my body lurched sideways like a rag being shaken loose from a line. My shoulder slammed into air that wasn't there long enough to catch me. The barrel skimmed past my ear — cold metal grazing skin — and then Cassian's elbow drove into Michael's ribs with the kind of precision that wasn't born from anger, but from training. Violence distilled into instinct. Not hesitation. Not mercy.

Michael grunted — more shock than pain — but he didn't fall.

Cassian made sure he did.

He grabbed a fistful of Michael's jacket and slammed him into the desk. Once. Twice. The wood groaned beneath the impact, the sound splitting the air like a bone giving way. Something cracked — maybe the desk. Maybe Michael. Maybe me.

Michael tried to recover, tried to swing the gun back toward us — but his arm was wild now, desperate instead of deliberate. Cassian's hand clamped around his wrist mid-aim and wrenched it sideways with brutal precision.

Michael's finger was still on the trigger.

The shot went off in the struggle — not aimed, not controlled

One deafening report. A burst of light. Burning air.

The recoil jolted the gun loose. It clattered across the floor.

For a second, I didn't understand what had happened.

I thought the ringing in my ears was from the gunshot—until I realized it was *me*, bleeding.

There was no pain yet. Just a numb pressure blooming along my side, like someone pressing a hot iron there and holding it steady. The heat spread. Then — just as quickly — came cold. Creeping in from the edges of the wound like frost claiming glass.

Voices exploded around me — radios crackling, officers shouting orders, boots crashing against the polished floor. Two cops lunged past me, tackling Michael to the ground. He hit the hardwood with a crash, cursing through clenched teeth as they pinned his arms behind his back and ground his cheek into the floor.

Nobody looked at me.

Nobody saw me.

Except him.

Cassian's head snapped toward me so fast it looked like his body had to catch up. His eyes — wild, feral for a heartbeat — found my hands pressed to my side. The red slicked through my fingers. The spreading warmth.

Color gone. Breath gone.

"Kennedy."

He was on me in two strides — a blur of heat and gravity — catching me just as my knees forgot how to hold me. His hands landed on me like he didn't know where to touch first — one on my back, steadying; one hovering, then pressing at my side with unbearable care.

"Hey. Hey. Look at me." His palm slid to the back of my neck, thumb anchoring under my jaw like he could physically keep my head from dropping. His forehead nearly touched mine, breath ragged and hot. His voice was too calm. Too leveled. Too deadly. "You're alright. You hear me? Stay with me."

I tried. God knows I tried. But the floor kept tilting. The room kept spinning, bending inward like the walls were folding me into darkness.

"We need help over here!" Cassian's voice cracked like a thunderclap, sharp enough to make even the cops flinch. "Now!"

Heads turned. Eyes widened. Someone swore. Someone moved.

But no one was fast enough for him.

His hand clamped harder over the wound, firm and unrelenting, like he could hold my blood inside through sheer force. He pulled me back into him, caging me against his chest — heart pounding against my spine — as if by proximity alone he could override whatever was happening inside me.

"I've got you," he said.

And there was nothing calm left in it.

Just a man — terrified — trying to stop the world from taking the only thing he was ever afraid to lose

Hands dragged Michael up from the floor, cuffs biting into his wrists as they yanked his arms behind his back. He didn't fight. Didn't plead. He stood like a man tolerating an inconvenience, not facing consequences. Two officers dragged him toward the door, their grips firm, but his posture still regal—spine straight, chin lifted, arrogance undisturbed.

He didn't look at Cassian. He looked at me. Not wild. Not enraged. Just… measured. Cold. Stripped of performance. His posture barely shifted, but his focus sharpened with surgical intent, like he was preparing to carve something out of me and wanted to be sure he made it clean. He leaned in — not far, just enough that the words would belong to *me* and no one else.

"Your mother ruined my life," he said, each syllable precise as a scalpel. "When she made me your father."

No flare. No venom. He didn't spit it or snarl it — he *delivered* it. Like an invoice. Like a statement of debt finally collected.

It didn't hit.

It settled.

Not like a blow. Like a verdict. Not shouted — stamped. Permanent.

If the bullet hadn't dropped me, his words almost did.

Somewhere beyond it, voices were moving — orders thrown, footsteps pounding, someone saying pressure on that side now — but it all sounded distant. Like it was happening in another room. Another world.

Everything inside me was split between two kinds of pain — the one burning through my side, and the one sinking, slow and decisive, into my chest.

When she made me your father.

My vision tunneled. The room swayed sideways, slow at first — then all at once.

Sound started to slip away next, like someone was turning the world down one dial at a time. Boots. Shouting. Even Cassian's voice — all muffled underwater. My body didn't feel like mine anymore. Too heavy. Too distant.

But his hands were still there.

One clamped over my blood-slick palm. The other braced against my back, holding me upright like he could will my spine to remember how to stand.

Everything began to dim — sound first, then light.

"Kennedy—" His voice cracked like something breaking open.

His mouth was still moving — begging, pleading, ordering — but I couldn't tell which.

I tried to answer anyway. I tried to hold onto him with the last breath I had.

"Cas—"

Cassian

21

"NO. No, no, no—" I adjusted my pressure on the wound, harder, crueler. I wanted it to hurt. I needed pain to keep her here. "Stay awake. I swear to God, Kennedy, look at me."

Someone said something behind me. A cop. A medic. I didn't register it.

Hands reached for her, and instinct took control before thought could intervene. I tightened my hold over the wound, leaning my body over hers like a shield. They could've shot me, dragged me off, tasered me — I wouldn't have moved.

"Back off," I growled without lifting my head.

"Sir, she needs—"

"I said back off."

My voice didn't rise, but something in it must have suggested violence, because the hands hovering near her hesitated. I didn't see who they belonged to — officer, medic, I didn't care. They were not touching her until I allowed it.

"Cassian!"

Sienna's voice cracked across the room like a snapped wire.

She was suddenly at my side, pale and streaked with tears, but fierce in a way only terror could forge.

"Move," she demanded, voice shaking but firm beneath it. "She needs help you *can't* give."

For a moment — one suspended, dangerous moment — I almost turned on her. The only thing standing between Kennedy and death was pressure, force, me. If I let go, I would lose her. I knew that with a certainty I had never applied to anything in my life.

But Sienna wasn't pleading for me to back down. She was pleading for Kennedy to live.

She was right.

And if I hesitated much longer, I'd kill her myself.

I eased back an inch at a time, slow and reluctant, like peeling my fingers off the edge of a cliff. The medic swooped in, pressing gauze and sealant foam where my hands had been. I stayed close — closer than I was supposed to — my palm still braced on her shoulder, my fingers trembling against her collarbone like I needed proof she was still warm.

They strapped her to a board. Her head tilted to the side, lips parted, lashes trembling like a wind was blowing through her veins instead of blood. She was still breathing — barely — and only because I willed it so.

"Family rides in the ambulance!"

Sienna didn't even wait for them to finish the sentence. She climbed in beside Kennedy and gripped her hand like she could drag her back to consciousness by sheer possession.

I stood there as the doors shut.

Her last breath — the one she tried to shape into my name — echoed in my skull.

Cas—

Barely a sound. Barely anything at all. And yet it felt like a whole life handed to me in a single broken syllable.

For one full second, I stood motionless in the wash of red and blue lights. Sirens blared. Radios crackled. Michael's curses bled down the hallway somewhere behind me. I didn't move. Couldn't. My mind kept replaying that one half-sound, that last look in her eyes before they closed.

Then my body remembered how to function.

I turned. Walked — not ran — to the car, luckily Sienna had left the keys on the seat. My hands were slick on the steering wheel, but I drove anyway. If the ambulance ran lights, I ran lights. If it weaved through traffic, I threaded the gaps before they even formed. The world blurred. My vision tunneled. There was only one destination: wherever they were taking her.

I parked badly — half on a curb — and was out of the car before the engine finished shuddering off. The hospital doors slid open, too slow, too calm for the moment. I pushed past anyone who spoke to me. Security. Nurse. Someone asking if I was injured. None of it mattered.

I followed the sound of wheels and beeping monitors until I caught sight of Sienna disappearing through double doors beside Kennedy's gurney. I tried to follow — caught a glimpse of blood-streaked gauze, pale skin, oxygen mask — before someone barred my path.

"Sir, you can't—"

I stared at the nurse like I had stared down death itself, and she stepped aside without finishing.

But another stopped me further down, firmer this time. They didn't care who I was or how I looked at them. They had rules. Protocols.

"She's going into surgery. You need to wait."

Wait.

As if time was something I still believed in.

As if seconds weren't weapons.

As if every tick of the clock didn't drain more of her life than that bullet already had.

I didn't argue. Not with words.

Just a man holding himself rigid, because if I let go in any direction — grief, rage, fear — I knew I would never come back from it.

I planted myself outside the operating room doors and stayed. Back to the wall, hands still stained, breath contained. People moved around me like I was background noise; I watched the hinge of those doors like it was the only thing left in the world that mattered. Time went on—somebody spoke, someone else laughed, a phone chimed—but it all happened somewhere beyond the edge of what I felt. All that lived in me in that long, flat stretch of waiting was one terrible, honest thing: if she dies, I do too.

Kennedy

22

Waking didn't happen cleanly. It came in slips and pieces, like surf shallowly washing over sand—touch, pull back, try again. The weight in my chest was the first thing I knew. Not pain yet; heaviness. Something mechanical kept count of me from somewhere to my left. The air smelled like antiseptic and old coffee, and the blanket over me had that hospital crispness that always felt like paper pretending to be soft.

When I opened my eyes, the room was dim. A single sconce threw warm light against a beige wall; shadows held the corners. The ceiling tiles were a grid I didn't recognize. The IV line at my wrist tugged when I shifted. Bandages pulled tight along my side and a dull ache answered everywhere at once, as if my body had tried to catalog every place that had been afraid.

A small bouquet sat on the tray beside the bed. Not the tidy, symmetrical kind nurses bring when they're trying to make a room look like a room. Stems cut unevenly, petals bruised at the edges, colors a little too dark for cheer. The card was blank, shoved under the vase like its presence was the only thing that mattered.

He was in the chair.

Head bowed, elbows on his knees, hands loosely clasped the way people pray when they don't know how. In the soft spill of light, I could see the split in Cassian's lower lip, the raw skin across his knuckles, the tired carved under his eyes like it had been chiseled there. His shirt was the same one—wrinkled past saving, dried patches darker than the fabric wanted to admit. The muscles along his forearms were relaxed in that way that meant nothing else in him was.

Something moved in me that I didn't approve of. Not soft. Not forgiving. A jolt, like my body knew him before my mind remembered why it shouldn't. The ache along my ribs sharpened when I breathed too deep. I let the breath out carefully.

I remembered what he said. What he was supposed to do.

He shouldn't have been here. Not after everything.
And yet, there he was.

The part of me that should've felt rage was too tired. The part that should've been grateful was too guarded. I didn't know what to feel, only that the sight of him—battered, hollow, waiting—unraveled something I wasn't ready to name.

I shifted. Just enough to make the mattress sigh.

His eyes snapped open.

Not groggy. Not startled. Immediate. Like he'd been waiting beneath the surface of sleep for any reason to break it.

For a moment, neither of us moved.

His gaze locked to mine with the kind of stillness that came from restraint, not calm. Every line in him went alert—but not to fight. To listen.

My throat worked before my voice could. "How long?"

"Three days." His voice held itself together like a man hauling weight by hand. "Surgery went well. The bullet missed anything they couldn't fix. You lost too much blood."

He swallowed. "You scared them."

You, not me. He didn't say it, but it lived in the space between us anyway.

"I should get the nurse," he added, already half rising.

"Wait." It came out quick, too small. I hated that. "Just... a minute."

He eased back into the chair like restraint physically hurt, like he'd shoved himself into stillness one muscle at a time. Up close, the split lip was worse; the skin over his knuckles had that shiny, healed-over sting, and there was a crescent of someone else's nail at the base of his thumb. The flowers on the tray made more sense. He hadn't known what to do with his hands.

Silence lay between us, not empty but heavy. The machines kept count of me. My pulse tried to match them and stumbled. My body remembered fear before it remembered safety.

Cassian's fingers flexed once against his knees. Then, slowly—like approaching a wounded animal—he reached. Not to touch, but to hover. His hand stopped above my wrist, close enough for his heat to register, far enough to honor what he thought he'd lost.

I could've pulled away. I could've let him hang there. I didn't.

Not forgiveness. Not decision. Just… choosing not to flinch.

"You stayed," I said quietly. Not accusation. Not thanks. Just fact.

"I'd never leave you." No apology. No plea. Just iron, stated like weather.

The words landed somewhere I wasn't ready to name. They hurt more than the stitches.

A flicker of motion drew my eye to the corner of the room. The television murmured low. Michael's face stared back from the screen—washed-out mugshot replacing his campaign smile. Charges scrolled across the bottom in white block text. The sound was too low to catch the details, but the headline was enough.

Cassian followed my gaze, then looked back to me, waiting for permission.

I nodded once.

He didn't reach for the remote with his hand still hovering above mine. He used the other. The volume clicked up.

"...denied bail this morning pending multiple felony counts, including conspiracy to commit murder," the anchor said. "According to officials, evidence was supplied by a third party and corroborated by court-authorized surveillance inside the Royal residence. Sources confirm...

Bugged. Of course. The lawyer's files had been the match. The house had been the kindling. The night had been the inferno.

My fingers curled against the sheets. The ceiling stayed still. The floor held. The world, for once, did not tilt.

"It's really over," I said. Not to him. To the room. To the wound. To the part of me that had been braced since childhood.

Cassian didn't rush the agreement.

"It's over," he said.

"And somehow you've made it sound like a beginning," I muttered.

His brows pulled in, confusion flickering across his face — not at the situation, but at *me.*

"For him," I continued, pulse climbing. "It's over for Michael. For the cops. For the city. But *not for us.*"

A breath caught in his chest. The kind you hear right before something breaks.

"Kennedy—"

"Don't." My voice frayed, harsher than I meant it. "Don't say my name like that. Like you have the right."

His jaw hardened. He didn't move toward me — but he didn't back away either. He held his position like a battlefield he refused to surrender.

"You think I *wanted* all this?" he asked, voice low, raw. "You think I don't know I lost that right?"

"You didn't lose it," I snapped. "You *sold* it."

The words hung between us like smoke. His nostrils flared — a hit taken straight to the ribs — but he didn't flinch. He absorbed it like he'd been preparing for every possible version of my hatred and agreed to endure each one.

"I know what I did," he said quietly.

"No, Cassian. I don't think you understand the damage that's been done." My fingers twisted into the blanket, anchoring me to the bed I suddenly despised. "You confessed like you wanted a standing ovation. Like honesty was enough to wipe out the fact that *you were supposed to kill me.*"

His eyes sparked — not with anger *at me* — but at the injustice of my words. Not because they were unfair. Because they were *accurate.*

"That's not it at all Kennedy," he said, voice sharpening into steel. "I confessed because I refused to let *him* write that story. I confessed because if you were going to run — or hate me — I wanted you to do it knowing my truth."

"Well congratulations," I bit out. "Mission accomplished."

Silence flexed — tight as wire.

He stepped closer — not enough to touch. Enough to *press.*

"You want me to fight?" he said, and there was something dangerous in the way he said it — not violent. Determined. "Fine. I'll fight. I would tear the world apart if it meant keeping you alive. You want anger? I have it. You want guilt? I live in it. But I won't apologize for wanting you to stay with me."

My breath shuddered. His voice wasn't loud. It didn't need to be.

He took another step.

"I wasn't hired to love you," he said, throat working. "But I do. And no bullet, no confession, no past makes that less real."

Tears threatened. I swallowed them down until they tasted like iron.

"Stop." My voice broke. "Stop saying things like that."

"Why?" he demanded. "Because it's easier to hate me?"

I went still. The room did too.

His chest heaved. Mine didn't know how.

He swallowed once. Twice. Then nodded — like he'd reached a line.

"If you want me gone, say it."

"I want—" My voice cracked in two. "I don't know what I want."

His expression changed — something raw and heartbreakingly soft flickering through stone.

"Yes, you do," he said gently. "You know. You just won't say it."

I couldn't answer. Couldn't tell him to stay. Couldn't tell him to go. Couldn't even breathe without feeling like I was choosing wrong.

His eyes softened just enough to make it worse.

"It's okay, Wildfire. I'll make it easy for you."

He stepped back—not in retreat, but in reverence. Like he was backing away from an altar he wasn't allowed to touch.

Every muscle in my body wanted to lurch after him. None of them obeyed.

He reached for the door. His hand rested on the handle for a heartbeat too long, like he was praying I'd stop him.

I didn't.

So he nodded once to himself—acceptance folded into resignation—and opened it.

Light from the hallway spilled across the floor. His silhouette cut through it.

Cassian didn't leave in anger. He didn't slam the door, didn't throw one last look over his shoulder like a wounded martyr. He simply stood there for a moment—silent, steady, unreadable—and obeyed me. He walked out because I told him to, because I forced him away with words I wasn't even sure I believed.

The door clicked shut.

The silence that followed wasn't peaceful. It was hollow. Too wide. Too loud. I stared at the space where he'd been standing, waiting for some sense of victory to arrive, some surge of righteous clarity to tell me I'd done the right thing.

It didn't come.

All that came was the sound of my own pulse, climbing higher with every second he stayed gone.

I told myself to breathe.

I couldn't.

Something inside me buckled—not thought, not logic, just instinct snapping like overstretched wire. My body moved before my pride could catch it. I tore the IV from my arm, barely wincing at the hot sting that followed, and swung my legs off the bed. The floor swayed when my feet touched it. I clung to the rail until the world steadied enough to stand on.

He was leaving.

And if I let him, that was it.

Not just the end of us.

The end of me.

I shoved the door open and stumbled into the hallway, one hand pressed to the bandage at my side, the other skimming along the wall to keep balance. Nurses called after me, distant and irrelevant. A monitor alarm wailed somewhere behind me, tattling on my escape. I ignored it all. My only focus was the soft echo of footsteps turning at the end of the corridor.

I rounded the corner—

And there he was.

Standing at the elevator, shoulders rigid, head bowed slightly like he was bracing himself to walk away from something he didn't know how to survive without. His hand hovered near the call button but didn't press it. Maybe he was waiting for me and just didn't know it.

"Cassian."

It wasn't loud. I didn't need it to be. His name left my mouth like a whisper, and he reacted as if it had been shouted.

His head lifted. His body stilled. For a moment neither of us moved. Not because we didn't want to—because movement felt too delicate for what was happening. His gaze locked onto mine with such intensity that the distance between us stopped feeling like space and started feeling like pressure.

He took one step forward.

And that was enough.

I didn't think. I pushed off the wall and walked toward him, every breath burning, every muscle protesting, but none of it enough to stop me. By the time I reached him, I didn't so much stop as collide—and he caught me automatically, instinctively, like gravity had just returned to its rightful direction.

His arm wrapped around my back. His other hand came up to steady my jaw like I might shatter if he wasn't careful.

"You shouldn't be out of bed," he said, voice low and wrecked.

"Then don't make me chase you," I breathed against his mouth.

His reply wasn't spoken.

It broke out of him like a confession too big for words.

He caught me—one hand at my jaw, the other at my waist, pulling me into him with a certainty that felt less like choice and more like gravity. His mouth crashed against mine, not soft, not careful, but steady—hungry without being reckless. The kind of kiss that didn't ask, didn't apologize, didn't pretend. The kind of kiss that planted its flag and dared the world to move it.

Every line of him pressed into me, and still it wasn't close enough. His chest against mine, his heartbeat slamming like it wanted to fuse with my ribs. His fingers curled, anchoring me like he thought I might vanish if he didn't hold hard enough.

And God, I let him. I let the weight of him pin me to something that finally felt like solid ground. My hands fisted in his shirt, not to pull him closer but to prove he was real, that he was here, that after everything, I could still touch him.

It wasn't gentle. It wasn't sweet. It was survival and surrender tangled up into one unbearable, unbreakable thing.

The elevator chimed behind him, interrupting our moment. He didn't turn as his lips continued to hover over mine.

"Come on," he said quietly, brushing his thumb once along my jaw. "You're going to pass out and make this dramatic."

I almost smiled.

Almost.

He steadied me back toward my room, one arm firm around my waist and settled me back into the bed with a patience that felt like penance. The nurse had scolded us—soft, practiced—then left on tiptoe with a stack of charts and a glare that said she'd seen stranger reconciliations before and lived to judge them. For a handful of minutes afterward the room smelled like antiseptic and the faint perfume of the flowers, and I let my eyes close because the world suddenly seemed thin enough to breathe.

When I opened them I looked for him the way you look for a light after a blackout. He was watching me, every line in his face softened the way stone softens under water. I wanted to tell him a thousand things then, but the words were all shapes behind my mouth.

My fingers found the vase because habit is a liturgy; I lifted the card as if I were pulling a small, skittish animal from its shelter. The paper made that intimate sound that means someone else had handled it first. Cassian's eyes followed the movement—quiet, careful, like he was afraid to break whatever this moment was trying to be.

"Who sent you the flowers?" he asked. His voice was soft, but tension lived underneath it—like even the wrong answer might reopen something they'd both fought to keep closed.

I smiled without meaning to. "I thought you did." The words came out smaller than I expected. Not teasing—just... tender. The kind of softness you forget you're allowed to have.

His jaw tightened in that way it does when he's trying not to show how much something matters. He didn't answer. Just watched me, patient, silent, the weight of everything unsaid pressing against the quiet.

I slid the envelope free. The handwriting was small, neat—careful in a way that made my chest twist. Someone who thought about every word before writing it. For a second, my thumb hovered over the flap, because there are tiny, stupid rituals you perform when you want control back. Then I opened it.

Cassian shifted, the chair creaking under him, waiting for whatever would follow. The paper felt warm from my hands, fragile in that way that meant it had come a long way to get here.

I read the first line and felt my breath catch. The second, and my pulse changed rhythm.

It wasn't cruel. It wasn't a threat. It was something else entirely—something that shouldn't have existed and yet somehow did.

There was no name at the top. No explanation. Just words from someone who, for the first time, wasn't a ghost.

So, I just found out you exist, and I can't stop thinking about it. About you. About everything you went through. I don't know what's true or who to believe yet, but I need you to know—I'm here. You're not alone in this anymore.
– Elara

The room tilted, quiet but full. I stared at the letter until the words blurred, until they didn't look like words at all—just pieces of something unfamiliar: hope, maybe.

Cassian didn't speak. He didn't need to. The silence between us was no longer empty; it felt like the start of something neither of us knew how to name yet.

I folded the letter once, twice, pressing the crease with my thumb before setting it down beside the bouquet of lilies.

For the first time in a long time, I didn't feel like someone's shadow.

Thank You

To the readers who have known darkness and still saw the light ahead— you are the heartbeat of this story.

To my husband, who gave me a love steady enough to heal old wounds and strong enough to carry new dreams. Thank you for being my home.

To my best friend— your honesty, your encouragement, and your unwavering belief in me helped shape every chapter.

And to everyone who picked up this book:
May you always remember that fire doesn't always mean destruction, sometimes it clears the way for something new.

The Author

Hailey M. Bertoldi writes romantic suspense stories that blend danger, emotion, and the kind of love that pulls you out of the dark. When she isn't writing, she can usually be found with an iced cold brew in hand, spending time with her husband and their four cats, or getting lost in a good book. She loves late-night writing sessions and getting swept up in the emotion of the stories she creates. *Wildfire* is her debut novel, and the beginning of many worlds she's excited to share.

Out of the flames and into the...

CROSS
FIRE

The flames may have been put out...

but the fallout has only begun.

Book Two of the Flames to Ashes Trilogy

Spring 2027